KU-491-271

PENGUIN BOOKS

BORDER CROSSING

'Compelling . . . hauntingly convincing. Few English writers now can match Barker's narrative poise, and she remains almost peerless in her articulation of the unspoken' *Observer*

'Intelligent and troubling . . . Barker's best book yet'
Literary Review

'A brave novel. Barker has squared up to some of the most intimidating of latter-day social issues. She refuses to be horrified by these issues, for to be horrified is to avert one's gaze . . . this is to be applauded'
The Times Literary Supplement

'A bold book . . . mercilessly acute, extraordinary, convincing' *Evening Standard*

'Disorientating and potentially horrifying . . . a taut psychological thriller, in which the reader's feelings of dread and danger are cranked up to the very last page . . . Barker delves unflinchingly into the enduring mysteries of human motivation' *Sunday Telegraph*

'Engrossing . . . straightforward and timely' *Economist*

ABOUT THE AUTHOR

Pat Barker was born in Thornaby-on-Tees in 1943. She was educated at the London School of Economics and has been a teacher of history and politics. Her books include *Union Street*, winner of the 1983 Fawcett Prize, which has been filmed as *Stanley and Iris*, *Blow Your House Down*, *Liza's England*, formerly *The Century's Daughter*, and the following published by Penguin: *The Man Who Wasn't There*; the highly acclaimed *Regeneration* trilogy, comprising *Regeneration*, *The Eye in the Door*, winner of the 1993 *Guardian* Fiction Prize, and *The Ghost Road*, winner of the 1995 Booker Prize for Fiction; *Another World*; and *Border Crossing*.

Pat Barker is married and lives in Durham.

PAT BARKER

Border Crossing

PENGUIN BOOKS

PENGUIN BOOKS

Published by the Penguin Group
Penguin Books Ltd, 80 Strand, London WC2R 0RL, England
Penguin Putnam Inc., 375 Hudson Street, New York, New York 10014, USA
Penguin Books Australia Ltd, 250 Camberwell Road, Camberwell, Victoria 3124, Australia
Penguin Books Canada Ltd, 10 Alcorn Avenue, Toronto, Ontario, Canada M4V 3B2
Penguin Books India (P) Ltd, 11, Community Centre, Panchsheel Park, New Delhi – 110 017, India
Penguin Books (NZ) Ltd, Cnr Rosedale and Airborne Roads, Albany, Auckland, New Zealand
Penguin Books (South Africa) (Pty) Ltd, 24 Sturdee Avenue, Rosebank 2196, South Africa

Penguin Books Ltd, Registered Offices: 80 Strand, London WC2R 0RL, England

www.penguin.com

First published by Viking 2001
Published in Penguin Books 2002

3

Copyright © Pat Barker, 2001
All rights reserved.

The extract on p. 249 from Myfanwy Piper's libretto of Benjamin
Britten's *The Turn of the Screw* appears by kind permission of Thrings & Long
Solicitors on behalf of the Estate of Myfanwy Piper

The moral right of the author has been asserted

Set in 11.5/14.5pt Monotype Bembo
Typeset by Rowland Phototypesetting Ltd, Bury St Edmunds, Suffolk
Printed in England by Clays Ltd, St Ives plc

For David

ONE

They were walking along the river path, away from the city, and as far as they knew they were alone.

They'd woken that morning to a curious stillness. Clouds sagged over the river, and there was mist like a sweat over the mud flats. The river had shrunk to its central channel, and seagulls skimmed low over the water. The colour was bleached out of houses and gardens and the clothes of the few passers-by.

They'd spent the morning indoors, picking away at their intractable problems, but then, just before lunch, Lauren had announced that she had to get out. They might have done better to drive to the coast, but instead they donned raincoats and boots and set off to walk along the river path.

They lived on the edge of what had once been a thriving area of docks, quays and warehouses, now derelict and awaiting demolition. Squatters had moved into some of the buildings. Others had suffered accidental or convenient fires, and were surrounded by barbed-wire fences, with pictures of Alsatians and notices saying DANGER. KEEP OUT.

Tom kept his eyes down, hearing Lauren's voice go on and on, as soft and insistent as the tides that, slapping against crumbling stone and rotting wood, worked bits of Newcastle loose. Keep talking, he said to clients who came to him for help in saving their marriages, or – rather more often – for permission to give up on them altogether. Now, faced with the breakdown of his own, he thought, Shut up, Lauren. Please, please, please shut up.

Bits of blue plastic, half-bricks, a seagull's torn-off wing. Tom's gaze was restricted to a few feet of pocked and pitted ground into which his feet intruded rhythmically. All other boundaries were gone. Though he did not raise his head to search for them, he was aware of their absence: the bridge, the opposite bank, the warehouses with the peeled and blistered names of those who had once owned them. All gone.

A gull, bigger and darker than the rest, flew over, and he raised his eyes to follow it. Perhaps this focus on the bird's flight explained why, in later years, when he looked back on that day, he remembered what he couldn't possibly have seen: a gull's eye view of the path. A man and a woman struggling along; the man striding ahead, eager to escape, hands thrust deep into the pockets of a black coat; the woman, fair-haired, wearing a beige coat that faded into the gravel, and talking, always talking. Though the red lips move, no sound comes out. He denies her his attention in memory, as he did in life. The perspective lengthens to include the whole scene, right up to the mist-shrouded warehouses that rise above them like cliffs, and now a third figure appears, coming out from between the derelict buildings.

He stops; looks towards the river, or rather at a small jetty that runs across the mud into the deep water, and starts to stride towards it. And at this moment, seeing in memory what in life he did not see, Tom freezes the frame.

In reality, it was Lauren who first noticed the young man. 'Look,' she said, touching Tom's arm.

They stood and watched him, grateful to be distracted from their own problems, to be mildly interested, mildly puzzled by the behaviour of another human being, for there was an oddity about this boy that they both recognized seconds before he did anything odd. His trainers bit into the gravel – the only sound except for their own breathing – and then he was slipping and slithering over the rotted timbers of the jetty. He stood, poised, at the end, a black shape smudged with mist. They watched him drop his coat, scrape off his trainers, tug the sweatshirt over his head.

'What's he doing?' Lauren said. 'He can't be going to swim.'

People did swim here: in summer you saw boys diving from the end of the jetty, but surely nobody would want to swim on a raw, murky day like this. He seemed to be shaking pills into the palm of his hand and cramming them into his mouth. He threw the bottle away, far out into the water, but his body got there first. A low, powerful dive that raised barely a splash. Almost immediately his head appeared, bobbing, as he was swept further from the bank.

Already Tom was running, crunching broken glass, dodging half-bricks, jumping piles of rubble. Once he lost his balance and almost fell, but immediately was up again and running, the slimy wood of the jetty treacherous beneath his feet.

At the end, fumbling with buttons, he looked down into the dead water, and thought, Shit. And realized this is what people do think who meet sudden, violent deaths. Shit. This is it. Oh bugger. Lauren came panting up and said nothing, not 'Don't' or 'Be careful' or anything like that, and he was grateful. 'It's September,' he said, answering one of the things she might have said, meaning the water wouldn't be lethally cold.

A second later, the water enclosed him in a coffin of ice. His mind contracted in fear, became a wordless pinprick of consciousness, as he fought the river that pushed him under, tossed him about, slapped him to and fro across the face, like an interrogator softening up his victim.

After the first few floundering strokes, he began to get used to the cold. At any rate he could get no colder. Looking around for the dark head, he realized he couldn't see it, and thought, Good, because now he could get out, phone the police, let them dredge the river or wait for the body to float. But then he saw the boy, drifting slowly with the current, thirty or forty feet away.

Water slopped into his mouth, skinning his throat, and then the current pushed him under. Bubbles of released breath trickled past his eyes. He kicked his way to the surface and came up closer to the boy. Purple face hidden by a fall of black hair. The current threatened to sweep Tom past, and he panicked, scrabbling at the water like a drowning dog. Then he let himself sink, and dimly, through the thick brown light, he saw the boy, hanging suspended, a dribble of bubbles escaping from his gaping mouth.

Tom grasped him by the arms and propelled him to the surface, gasping for air as they broke through and floated, the sky rocking around their drifting heads. Deep breaths. The river seemed to squeeze his chest tight. He didn't care, now, whether the boy was alive or dead. The determination to get him out had become as mindless as a dog's retrieving of a stick. The current made the turn difficult, but then he saw Lauren running along the path, and, towing the boy along, his eyes full of sky and river water, he struck out towards the bank. He made slow progress at first, then, miraculously, felt the tug of another current pulling them in to land. They floated, at last, into a fetid backwater, amongst a scum of rubbish the tide had cast up. A shopping trolley, knotted condoms, tinfoil trays, plastic bottles.

Tom pushed his face through it, to reach the edge of the mud. Thick, black, oily, stinking mud, not the inert stuff you encounter in country lanes and scrape off your boots at the end of the day, but a sucking quagmire, God knows how many feet deep. Lauren reached out to him.

'Don't come in,' he shouted.

A tree had been washed up on to the bank, and she clung to that, reaching out her hand. He began to inch his way towards her, keeping his weight evenly spread, dragging the boy behind him. The mud clutched at his elbows and knees. Lauren's spread fingers seemed a mile away, and she wouldn't have the strength to pull them out even if he managed to reach her. The stench and taste of the mud filled his nose and mouth. He was aware of not wanting to die and, quite specifically, of not wanting to die like this. Heart shaking his chest, he squirmed forward, and found the new ground firmer than he'd thought. Lauren, still clinging to the dead tree, had waded in to her knees. His outstretched fingers closed over hers, and slipped. 'Get my sleeve,' she said. He knew he should be keeping the boy's mouth clear, but there was no way he could do that and drag him out at the same time. Another few inches and he was able to grab Lauren's coat. The effort exhausted him and he lay still, panting for a while, then started to crawl across her until his hand closed round a branch of the tree. He tested it, found it locked fast in a groyne of the bank, and slowly stood up, hauling the boy behind him out of the mud, which surrendered him with a belch of protest. Tom lay gasping, head and shoulders on the grass, feet trailing in the slime. Then he told himself the job wasn't done, and turned to look at the boy.

Black and glistening, he lay there, a creature formed, apparently, of mud. Lauren knelt beside him, supporting his head, while Tom raked an index finger round the inside of his mouth, checking that the airways were clear. Then he pressed two fingers against the slimy neck, but his hands were so numb with cold that he couldn't feel anything. He shifted his hold, dug deeper.

'Yes?' Lauren said.

'No.'

'Shit.'

Immediately she placed her hands one on top of the other on the boy's breastbone, and pressed down. Tom tilted the head back and – aware of a momentary frisson of distaste that surprised him – pinched the nose, fastened his mouth over the flaccid lips and blew. Through the spread fingers of his left hand he felt the ribcage rise, then he came up for breath, counted, went down again. The boy's mouth jerked under his, as Lauren pressed again. He heard her grunt with effort. This time when he came up he looked at her. Her eyes were glazed, inward-looking. Like labour, Tom thought, the irony as sour as the mud on his tongue. The boy looked like a baby: purple face, wet hair, that drowned look of the newborn, cast up on to its mother's suddenly creased and spongy belly. Distracted by thoughts and memories, Tom breathed too hard, detected from a struggle in the boy's chest that the rhythm had been lost, checked himself, counted, went down again. His breath snagged in the boy's throat. He pressed his fingers to the carotid again and thought he detected a flutter. 'Got him.'

They waited, Lauren's hands still clasped one on top of the other, ready to start again. One breath, then another. And another. No way of telling whether the colour was coming back. His face was masked by mud.

'All right,' Lauren said. 'Let's get him over.'

Together they heaved him into the recovery position. She stood up, brushing pebbles from her knees, and looked up and down the path, but the damp fog was enough to keep people indoors and there was nobody to send for help.

'It's probably quicker for me to run back to the house,' she said.

'No, I'll go.'

'I think you'd better stay where you are.'

Something in her voice startled him. He looked down and realized he was wearing a red glove. The

8

blood had dried on his fingers, which felt tight and sticky. He had no memory of injuring himself, and felt no pain, but he must have seemed shaky, because Lauren said, 'Are you sure you'll be all right?'

'Yes, go on.'

He watched her set off down the road, a tall, pale, blonde figure fading rapidly into the mist, which had thickened and lay over everything, smelling metallic, iron perhaps, unless that was the blood on his hand. The boy's eyes were closed. Tom took his pulse, and then, hobbling over the sharp gravel, retraced his steps to the end of the jetty, and picked up his coat and the little heap of the boy's clothes. Then he stood still for a moment, looking out over the water. The mud smelt sharp and strong. He was conscious of his skin chafing against his wet clothes, and he was filled with joy.

The elation drained away as he walked back, tripping over dangling sleeves like a honeymooner in an old-fashioned farce. The cut on his arm had begun to ache. He knelt down beside the boy, wrapped the heavier of the coats round him, then huddled inside the other, muttering under his breath as he rocked to and fro: C'mon, Lauren. C'mon. He was too cold to think or feel anything.

After a few minutes he heard an engine, then voices. He looked up to see two black-clad paramedics negotiating a stretcher down the crumbling steps. They worked their way along the bank, elbowing branches of willow aside. Thank God, he could sign off now, have a hot bath, a whisky, two whiskies, climb back inside his own life.

A stocky woman with strongly marked eyebrows reached him first, followed by a bull-necked man with a ginger moustache, still breathless from the struggle to get the stretcher down the steps.

'My God,' the woman said, kneeling down. 'Wasn't your Saturday morning, was it, son?'

They worked quickly. Within minutes they'd re-moved the coat, checked his pulse and breathing, wrapped blankets round him, established that neither Tom nor Lauren knew who he was.

'We were just going for a walk,' Lauren said.

'Lucky for him you were.'

Gently, they transferred him to the stretcher. The small procession filed along the bank. The boy's head was hidden now, wrapped in the folds of a red blanket: a solitary splash of colour against the waste of black mud. When they reached the steps, Tom pushed his way forward and helped discreetly with the lifting. The mud on the boy's face had begun to dry and crack, like a ritual mask or the worst case of psoriasis you could imagine.

The ambulance was parked a short way from the steps. They trudged over the gravel and set him down briefly on the ground while they opened the doors. At the last moment, just as they were preparing to slot the stretcher in, the boy stirred and groaned.

'You'll be all right,' Tom said, touching his shoulder, but there was no sign that he'd heard.

'You want to get that cut looked at,' the woman said, gesturing at Tom's arm. 'We could take you in now, you know, if you liked.'

'No, it's all right, thanks. I'll see my own doctor.'

'Where are you taking him?' Lauren asked.

'The General.'

The engine was running. Tom bundled the boy's clothes together and handed them up to the woman. The doors slammed shut. Tom and Lauren stood and watched as the ambulance jolted along the path, weaving from side to side to avoid the worst of the potholes, and then, reaching smooth tarmac, accelerated, and disappeared round a bend in the road.

TWO

After the ambulance had gone, Tom went back to the jetty and, kneeling at the far end, managed to scoop up enough water to wash off the worst of the mud. A smell came off the river: something cold, fishy and rotten – and then he realized it was coming, not only from the water, but from his clothes, his skin, his hair.

They didn't speak at all on the way back. He hadn't bothered to put his trainers on and the pebbles hurt his feet. As soon as they were in the house, Lauren took him upstairs to have a look at the cut. 'It's not too bad,' she said, peering down at it.

'They always look worse than they are,' he said, impatient to have it over.

She washed his arm with a sterile solution, till the sides of the small wound gaped white, then pressed the edges together and applied a clear, waterproof dressing. She didn't speak as she worked and was breathing audibly, as children do when they concentrate. A dim memory of playing doctors and nurses with his slightly older girl cousins came back to him. He'd always been the patient, he remembered, though in those far-off games it had never been his arm that required attention. There was something erotic in Lauren's intent, impersonal gaze, and he put his free hand on her hip.

'Hot bath,' Lauren said, closing the lid of the first-aid box. 'Do you a lot more good than whisky.'

Resigned, he stripped off his wet clothes. She was bending over the bath, stirring the water, her face slick with steam. 'Do you think he'll be all right?'

'Depends what he took. Prozac, yes. Paracetamol, no.'

'Do you think we should ring?'

'No,' he said. 'We did what we could. It's somebody else's problem now.'

'I'll put these into wash,' she said, picking up his clothes.

He could see she was disappointed. She'd wanted to talk, to polish the shared-but-different experience until it acquired an even patina, became theirs, rather than his and hers. But he was used to switching off, to living his life in separate compartments. He'd learnt early, in his first few months of practice, that those who take the misery home with them burn out and end up no use to anybody. He'd learnt to value detachment: the clinician's splinter of ice in the heart. Only much later had he learnt to distrust it too – its capacity to grow and take over the personality. *Splinter* of ice?

He'd had colleagues who could have sunk the *Titanic*.

Gingerly, he lowered his aching shoulders into the water. Looking along the length of his body, he saw his cock, slightly engorged from the heat, gleaming and bobbing in the foam like a cylindrical fish. Well, he*llo*, there, he thought, slipping into the mid-Atlantic drawl he used to distance pain.

'Are you any warmer?' Lauren asked, coming back with an armful of towels.

'Bit. Why don't you get in? You must be frozen.'

Dropping her clothes in a heap near the door, she climbed into the bath behind him, and lowered herself cautiously into the water. 'Ouch.'

'Sorry.' He kept forgetting his 'hot bath' was Lauren's idea of being boiled alive. 'Would you like more cold?'

'No, it's all right. I'm in now.'

Her breath came in little explosive bursts against his back. He could feel her breasts pressing against his shoulder blades, and then her hand crept round, burrowing between his legs until she found, and cradled, his balls.

'Not fair,' he said. 'I can't reach anything.'

Groping under his arm, he found a nipple, and felt her laughter vibrate in his chest. A flash memory of cold mud sucking him in. 'C'mon,' he said. 'Let's go to bed.'

They dried each other, then he chased her upstairs, and they fell on to the bed, where they lay, gasping for breath. Her eye, an inch away from his, was a grey fish caught in a mesh of lines. For the first time in months he didn't know or care where she was in her cycle. This had nothing to do with ovulation or getting her pregnant, and not much to do, if he were honest, with loving her. Everything to do with the moment when he'd seen the boy's body hang suspended, like a specimen in a jar of formaldehyde, an umbilical cord of silver bubbles linking his slack mouth to the air. He saw him now. The boundaries of flesh and bone seemed to vanish. He was staring at his own death.

Afterwards they lay side by side, a medieval knight and lady on a tomb.

'I'm sorry,' he said. He knew she hadn't come.

'It's all right.'

He felt the bed shaking and knew she'd started to cry. 'Lauren . . .'

She sat up. 'Do you realize you risked your life back there for a complete fucking stranger?'

If this had been said with a scintilla of admiration, he'd have felt obliged to pooh-pooh the idea, to point out that he swam further than that every other day of his life, but her tone was aggressive, and he matched it. 'There was no choice.'

A stubborn silence.

'If I wasn't a strong swimmer, I wouldn't have gone in. But I am. And, anyway, I'm all right.'

She wasn't angry with him for diving into the river.

She was angry about the botched sex, and about his failure to get her pregnant. 'Let's have a drink, shall we?'

He didn't expect her to follow him downstairs, and she didn't. If only getting pregnant hadn't become such an obsession. She reminded him of one of those female fish that, in times of environmental hardship, dispense with the male sex altogether, and carry his gonads in a purse on their sides. Well, sod that, he thought, glugging whisky. He was fed up to the back teeth with being a walking, talking sperm bank.

His mother (not that she knew the details, thank God!) blamed their difficulties on the new pattern of their lives. For the past year Lauren had been working in London, teaching at St Margaret's School of Art, coming home only at weekends. 'Husband and wife should stick together,' his mother had said, sniffing over the tea towel she was using to polish a glass. 'You and Dad were apart when he was in the army.' 'And a fat lot of good it did us,' she flashed back at him.

But marriage was different now, he told her. Women didn't expect to sacrifice their careers to their husbands.

'Marriage doesn't change as much as you think,' she said, with another sniff. 'You'd be better off sticking together.'

At the time he'd dismissed her as old-fashioned. Now it didn't seem as simple as that. In his bleaker moments, he wondered whether he and Lauren hadn't separated already, without even letting themselves know they were doing it. He could have gone to London with her. He was on sabbatical at the moment, writing up a three-year research project, and books can be written anywhere. There would have been nothing to stop him e-mailing chapters to his colleagues for comment, and if he had needed a face-to-face meeting he could have come back for a few days, or overnight. He hadn't gone because he wanted to stay here. And since then, month by month, the sex had deteriorated. He blamed thermometers, calendars and pots of urine, and okay, he did find them a total turn-off, but there was something else he wasn't admitting. Perhaps he'd just voted with . . . Well. Not with his feet.

'Why?' Lauren asked, after one of his not infrequent failures.

'I don't know.'

But she was having no truck with that. He was a psychologist, for Christ's sake. It was his job to know.

He'd downed one tumbler of whisky, and was starting on the next, when Lauren came into the kitchen, and wrapped her arms around him. 'Look,' she said. 'What you did was very brave and I'm sorry.'

'What for?'

'For hating you for doing it.'

Suddenly they were both laughing, and, for a few moments, it was all right.

★

It was late evening before he remembered the post. He'd left the house yesterday in a tremendous hurry because he'd thought he was going to be late for Lauren's train, and didn't want to leave her stranded at the station. The postman had met him a few yards from the front door and handed him the mail. Without bothering to glance at it, he'd shoved it into his coat pocket, and then, absorbed in discussing the difficulties of the marriage, he'd forgotten all about it.

Lauren was loading the dishwasher. 'Where did you put my coat, darling?' he called downstairs.

'Utility room.'

As soon as he lifted it off the peg, he knew. River mud and, mixed in with that, a whiff of stale tobacco. He thrust his hand into the right pocket and pulled out a packet of cigarettes. It was immediately obvious what had happened. He'd wrapped his own coat round the boy, because it was heavier, and that was the one he'd handed into the ambulance. He couldn't put off trying to get it back, because there were spare keys in the pocket, and oh God, yes, his address on the envelopes. Admittedly, the boy wasn't in much of a state to contemplate burglary, but you didn't know. You didn't know who or what he was. He could be a drug addict desperate for cash.

'I seem to've got the wrong coat, darling. I'll have to go to the hospital.'

'Can't it wait?'

'Well, no, not really. There were letters in it.'

He didn't want to alarm her by mentioning the keys.

It was only a short drive to the General, but then he had to spend fifteen minutes trying to find somewhere to park. Visiting hour. Cars crammed bumper to bumper in every legitimate, and illegitimate, space.

The casualty department was packed. On a bench near the door a boy with a torn ear and blood trickling down his neck stared around with a kind of blank belligerence. A short distance away a young boy, his voice shooting up into registers he never intended, was trying to calm down a middle-aged woman. 'Howay, Mam. Don't let him see you upset.' '*Upset?* I'll give him bloody upset . . .' On a trolley near by, an old man, with a miner's blue scars on the backs of his hands, gasped his life away.

'Ward Eighteen,' a nurse said, raising her head, briefly, between disasters.

He walked the length of the corridor to Ward Eighteen and stopped by the nurses' station. An old man in a wheelchair, at the entrance to one of the wards, grabbed a nurse's behind as she walked past. 'Now then, Jimmy,' she said. 'You be a good lad now.' The old man cackled in demented glee, and pawed another nurse. They'll trank the life out of you, old son, Tom thought, if you don't behave.

A tall, rangy woman with strands of ultra-fine hair escaping from a knot on the top of her head, glasses dangling from a gold chain, and a general air of equine goodwill squeaked up to him on rubber-soled shoes. 'Tom. Hello!'

Mary Peters. He couldn't have wished for anyone better. 'Hello, Mary. I'm looking for an attempted suicide you had brought in this morning. Quite a young lad.'

She twinkled at him. 'Oh yes, I know. One of yours?'

'No, this isn't a professional visit, actually.' He felt embarrassed. 'I'm the one who fished him out. Only in the process he ended up with my coat. And I got his.'

'Yes, we found your coat. And the letters. You're lucky,' she said, leading the way down the corridor. 'The nurse read the name and address on the envelopes and assumed it was his name. You were very nearly admitted.' She stopped in front of a door. 'Fortunately he came round in time. His name's Ian Wilkinson.' She tapped her throat. 'And he won't feel like talking.'

'What did he take?'

'Temazepam. About ten, he thinks.'

The young man lying in the bed stared at Tom, the colour draining from his face. Tom was puzzled by the reaction, and by his own sense that he knew this boy. Of course he dealt with hundreds of disturbed young people in the course of a year . . . Still, he generally remembered them. He wasn't good with faces, but he remembered names. Ian Wilkinson. It meant nothing.

'This is Dr Seymour,' Mary said. 'Who rescued you. I don't suppose you . . .' Her voice died away, as she registered the atmosphere in the room. 'Well,' she said, after a slight pause. 'I'll leave you to it, then.' At the door she turned. 'Coat in the locker, Tom, when you're ready.'

'Thanks,' he said, shifting his gaze in time to see the door close.

The boy was hauling himself up the bed as if his first impulse were to escape. His colour hadn't returned. 'You don't recognize me, do you?' he said. 'I suppose I ought to find that reassuring.'

'You were covered in mud.'

'No, I mean before.' His voice was hoarse. 'When I was ten. Do you remember, you –'

Oh my God, Tom thought. He sat down heavily on the chair beside the bed. 'Danny Miller.'

'That's right.'

Saying the name changed his perception of the face. Now, second by second, under the sharp bones and planes of the adult face, a child's rounded, pre-pubescent features rose to the surface, and broke through, like a long-submerged body. 'I'm sorry,' Tom said. 'I didn't even know you were out.'

'It was kept pretty quiet, as you can imagine. And . . .' He nodded towards the door.

'Yes, of course. New name.'

'Ian was the governor's second name. Wilkinson was the chaplain's mother's maiden name.' His voice was expressionless.

'How long have you been out?'

'Ten months.'

'I won't ask how it's going.'

Danny – he couldn't think of him as Ian – looked startled for a moment, then burst out laughing. A second later he was pressing his throat. 'Tube.'

'It'll be sore for a few days.'

When Danny could speak again, he said, 'What do you reckon the chances are of this happening?'

'Of our meeting like this? A million to one.'

'Makes you think, doesn't it?'

It certainly did. Tom was already wondering whether this was genuine coincidence, or a dramatic gesture gone badly, almost fatally, wrong. Dramatic gestures of that kind are not uncommon, and they very frequently do go wrong, because the people making them usually have spectacularly flawed judgement. But to believe the meeting had been intended, he'd have to believe that Danny, for some undisclosed reason, had located him, and then, instead of ringing the doorbell, had decided to introduce himself by jumping into the river. It made no sense.

'You know, when something like this happens,' Danny said, 'it makes you realize things aren't just random. There is a purpose.'

Yes, possibly, Tom thought. But whose? 'It doesn't make me think that.'

'You know the chaplain I just mentioned? He used to say coincidence is the crack in human affairs that lets God or the Devil in.'

Tom smiled. 'I think what we need to let into human affairs is a bit more rationality.'

A pause. They seemed to have got in very deep, very quickly. Almost as if he'd read Tom's thoughts, Danny said, 'At least we're not talking about the weather while you eat all the grapes.'

There were no grapes. No visitors. Nothing. Looking round the bleak, bare room, Tom knew it was impossible just to take his coat and go. 'When do they say you'll be out?'

'Tomorrow.'

'Will you go home?'

'No, I'm in a bedsit. I'm a student.'

'What're you reading?'

'English.'

'Do you have somebody you can talk to?'

A shrug. 'My probation officer. Martha Pitt.'

'Oh yes, I know Martha. Shall I give her a ring and tell her you're here?'

'No, don't bother, it's the weekend. She has enough trouble with me. She was trailing over the Pennines last weekend to come and get me. I ran away to prison.'

'You went back to prison?'

'Yeah, I know. Sounds mad, doesn't it?'

'What happened?'

'They told me to bugger off. And then the governor rang Martha, and she came and got me.'

'Was that when you –'

'Decided to go for a swim? No.' He looked away. 'I don't know. Perhaps it was. It certainly didn't help.'

Tom thought for a moment. 'You know, you could come and talk to me, if you think it would be useful. Nothing formal. Just a chat.'

Danny smiled. 'About old times?'

'Whatever.'

The smile faded. 'Yes, I would like to.'

'I'll give you the address.' Tearing a page from the back of his diary, Tom wrote it down, adding, as an afterthought, his telephone number. He'd better make it an early appointment, so Danny had a date to look forward to. Discharge from hospital after a suicide attempt was a dangerous time. 'Shall we say Tuesday evening, about eight o'clock? And if anything goes wrong, you can give me a ring.'

'Thanks.' Danny folded the page. 'Your letters are in the locker. I was going to return them. And the coat.'

Defensive now, anxious to assert his honesty. Well, he did have twelve years in secure accommodation to live down. More than half his life. What had they made of him? What had they done with him? Part of Tom's interest was simple professional curiosity. It wasn't often you got the chance to follow up a case like Danny's, but he was also concerned for this unknown young man whose face and personality seemed to contain, untouched, the child he had once been.

Tom got his coat from the locker, releasing, in the process, a powerful smell of river mud and decay.

'You won't be wearing that before it's cleaned.'

'You won't be wearing this either,' Tom said, bundling Danny's coat into the locker. 'Well, then. See you Tuesday.'

Danny raised a hand, but he'd fallen back against the pillows, and seemed unable to speak. Tom closed the door quietly behind him.

Mary Peters was standing by the desk, talking to the ward sister, and it seemed only polite to pause and say goodbye.

'Well, what was all that about?' she asked.

'Oh, nothing much. He turned out to be an old patient. Hadn't seen him for years.'

She seemed satisfied. And Danny *had* changed. There was no reason to suppose he'd be recognized by anybody who'd only seen his school photograph in the papers or on TV, thirteen years ago. After all, he hadn't recognized him, and his contact with Danny went well beyond that.

Walking across the car park, he felt dazed, and stopped for a moment under the tarnished trees. He was remembering another car park, in June, in a heat wave. Arriving at the remand centre, where Danny was being held, twenty minutes before the time of his appointment, he'd chosen to wait outside, rather than in some dreary room inside the prison. The sun beat down and the car quickly became an oven. He left the doors open, and walked up and down the perimeter fence, listening to a Test Match on the radio. He had no need to familiarize himself with the notes spilling out of the files on the back seat. He knew them almost off by heart, and, in a sense, his task now was to forget them. The main pitfall in assessing the mental state of an offender is to produce a report that fits the crime, rather than the symptoms of the particular individual who is alleged to have committed it.

Sweat from the long journey evaporated from his armpits and groin. He was surrounded by beds of red-hot pokers, hundreds of them, coral-pink and gold spires proudly erect or drooping, at detumescent angles, over the path. A ripple of decorous applause came from the car radio. His mind filled with images from the path-lab photographs – Lizzie Parks's body laid out on the slab. It seemed incredible that a child should have done that. He went on pacing, up and down, up and down, and the red-hot pokers seemed to breathe in his horror and incredulity, and exhale them as heat and dust.

And here Danny was, thirteen years later, grown up, out of prison, living under a false identity supplied by the Home Office and the police. He couldn't tell Lauren. Any more than Martha Pitt had been able to tell him, though they were colleagues on the Youth Violence Project and saw each other at least once a week. She'd been supervising Danny for months. She knew Tom had been involved in his trial, but she hadn't once mentioned him. Well, good for Martha. That was the degree of secrecy required.

He walked across to his car, deactivated the alarm and opened the door. 'Coincidence is the crack in human affairs that lets God or the Devil in.' Typical God-bothering rubbish, he thought, though his own paranoid suspicion that Danny had plotted the meeting was no more rational. The fact is, that when confronted by a number of disturbing events, the human mind insists on finding a pattern. We can't wait to thread the black beads on to a single string. But some events are, simply, random.

Perhaps. Adjusting the mirror, he caught his own eye in the glass, and stared back at himself, alert, sceptical, unconsoled.

THREE

In the railway-station buffet, at eight o'clock on Monday morning, Lauren sat hunched over a table, spearing worms of ash on a burnt matchstick. 'I just think we need help.'

'You mean I need help.'

'We're not making love often enough, are we?'

'We're not "making love" at all.' He tried not to sound bitter. 'Look, why don't we give it a bit more time?'

'I haven't got time.'

'We, Lauren. We haven't got time.'

She shook her head. 'But that's the point, isn't it? The clock isn't ticking for you. You'll still be spraying tiddlers round all over the place when you're eighty.'

Not on present showing, he thought. 'What I think about going for help is that it's going to focus even more attention on the problem, and I think that's the trouble, you see. We've become . . . obsessed.'

'You mean I have.'

'All right, yes, you. I'm sick of being a sperm bank. I'm sick of feeling I don't count. What's happened to the, to the . . . relationship, for God's sake?' He leant towards her. 'When we got married, you didn't even want kids. It was . . . you and me.'

An incomprehensible announcement blared out of the loudspeaker above their heads. 'I've got to go,' she said.

'Ring me tonight.'

She pushed a strand of pale-blonde hair behind her ear. 'I don't know what I'm doing tonight.'

They walked across the bridge in silence. On the platform he asked, 'Are you coming home next weekend?'

'No, I'm going to my parents. I told you, don't you remember?'

After that they stood in silence, not looking at each other, until the train came in.

Back home, Tom pulled the duvet up over the creased sheet, the scene of his most recent failure, the one they couldn't ignore. He wished he had the energy to change the sheets, because he knew that tonight, when he got into bed, they'd smell of Lauren's scent, and he was beginning to dislike it. It seemed to him cloying, over-sensuous, now, though he'd loved it once, when he still loved her. And then he was horror struck, standing there, staring into the mirror, a pillow in his hands, because he'd trapped himself into using the past tense.

He did love her. They were in trouble, yes, but he was never sure how much trouble. Only nine months ago – telling themselves that a delay in conceiving was only to be expected at her age – they'd been happy. There were many times when that happiness still flickered over the surface of their present lives, and it seemed possible to grasp it again. Not just possible – easy. And yet they never quite managed it.

He made coffee and took it up to his study. He'd chosen to work in one of the attic rooms on the top floor because he loved the view of the river, though most mornings he had to wipe a hole in the condensation on the glass before he could see it. Not much of a view today. The sea fret had lasted all weekend, and the arch of the bridge rose out of the mist, disconnected from road and river, as apparently functionless as Stonehenge.

To work. His current task was to read through the fictionalized case histories he'd used in the book to check that they were sufficiently different from the originals to protect children's identities. Most of them he hadn't seen for months, though their voices were preserved on tape.

Michelle. Ten years old. Included in the research cohort – she was the only girl – because she'd bitten off the nose of her foster mother's natural daughter.

'Why did you do that?' Tom had asked, the first time they met.

' 'Cos she was slagging off me mam.'

A bold, self-confident expression, the abused child's air of knowing exactly what was what and how much you had to pay for it. He was sure she'd have rated her chances of getting him to take his trousers off, right there on the floor of the consulting room, very high indeed. Nothing a man was capable of would have surprised Michelle, except restraint.

She'd used the word 'justice' seven times in the course of their first interview, and that intrigued him. Her teachers rated her ability as average, at best. By no stretch of the imagination was Michelle an 'academic' child, and yet she kept returning to this abstract concept.

'He was an animal,' she said, referring to her mother's boyfriend, who'd raped her when she was eight. 'It wasn't just me, he had a go at me nanna 'n' all – and the dog.'

'Did it bite him?' Tom asked.

She looked at him suspiciously, afraid he might be laughing at her. 'No, but I did. And then me mam went into hospital, and she hadn't to have any drink, with her liver 'n' all that, and he poured vodka into the orange juice. I watched him do it. He could've killed her. He used to come in drunk and beat her up, and I used to wait for him in the kitchen with the lights out, leave the back window open, and as soon as he got his fingers on the sill I'd jump up and slam it down. It was great, that.' Her smile faded. 'Only then I got took into care.'

'Do you remember why you were taken into care?'

Michelle lowered her head.

'Do you know why?'

' 'Cos me mam brayed us.'

'Why did she do that?'

' 'Cos she didn't believe us.'

'About him raping you?'

'Yeah, she says I was making it up, but I wasn't.'

'No, I know you weren't.'

'She still won't have it, you know. Sun rises and sets out of his bloody arsehole. It's not fair.'

'What isn't?'

'Him. Two bloody years, time off for good behaviour, bounces back out like a frigging yo-yo. I lost me mam, me baby brother – I used to put him to bed every night, but he's only two, he won't remember – and the poor bloody dog got put down. She says she couldn't stand to see it after what I'd said. Now where's the justice in that?'

'Didn't she believe your nanna?'

'Nah, she just says women her age get fancying.'

Tom needed Michelle for the discussion on moral thinking in children with conduct disorder. It was too easily assumed that such children simply lacked conscience. Of course, a minority did. Preserved on tape, somewhere in the box, was Jason Hargreave saying, in his piping treble, 'Conscience is a little man inside your head that tells you not to do things. Only I haven't got one.' Four people had died in the fire

Jason started, and he had shown not a hint of remorse. But Jason wasn't typical. Michelle, in everything but gender, was. Many of the children, and most of the adolescents he talked to, were preoccupied – no, obsessed – with issues of loyalty, betrayal, justice, rights (theirs), courage, cowardice, reputation, shame. Theirs was a warrior morality, primitive and exacting. Nothing much in common with the values of mainstream society, but then they came from places that had been pushed to the edge: sink housing estates, urban ghettos. The young men were unemployed, sexually active, took little responsibility for their children (though their mothers often did), and cared more for the reputation of being 'hard' than for anything else. They were warriors. The little boys in the research project knew that this was the future, and sensibly prepared for it. School was irrelevant – and most of them didn't go.

Tom worked for three hours, clicked Print, then set off to the hospital where he'd arranged to meet Roddy Taylor for lunch. Roddy was the director of the eighteen-bed, medium-secure unit that currently housed Michelle.

Roddy was larger than life, irrepressible, Henry the Eighth in a pinstripe suit, and running late, as usual. He looked up as Tom entered the room.

'One more call, and I'm with you.'

Tom put the sheaf of papers on his desk, and sat down.

'Is that moral perception?' Roddy asked, while waiting to be connected.

'Yes –'

Roddy held his hand up, listening intently. 'All right, then, send him in.' More listening. 'Yes, yes. Yes, I know.' He put the phone down. 'Do you know, I honestly believe they think hospital beds breed like rabbits. Anyway –'

'This still isn't the final draft, but it's readable, I think. There's three of yours in there. Michelle, Jason, Brian.'

They talked about the cases for a while, then Roddy stood up and lifted his jacket off the back of the chair. 'C'mon, let's walk, shall we? I could do with a breath of fresh air.'

The pub was five minutes away, across a public square where young people lay sunbathing on the grass. A girl, with slim, brown, muscular arms and cropped, bleached-blonde hair, lay close to the path. 'Will you look at the tits on that?' Roddy muttered, as they walked past, hardly bothering to disguise his lust. With his huge, flapping bags of trousers, he looked much older than his forty years. He had three children now, and he spent most of his working life with younger people. But at least he knew where he was in the generations. One of Tom's fears was that people who remain childless never really grow up. When he thought of the childless marriages he knew, it seemed to him that, in almost every instance, one of the partners had become the child. Somewhere, in the distance, was a vision of total selfishness, that dreadful, terminal boyishness of men who can't stop thinking of themselves as young.

Tom had watched Lauren, tears streaming down her face, wrapping a christening present for Toby, Roddy and Angela's youngest child. 'Don't let's go, Lauren,' he'd said. 'We don't have to.' 'Yes, we do,' she'd said, and of course she was right. All their friends had children now. Either they adjusted to the fact and tried to fit in, or they spent their lives, isolated, in a child-free zone. He made a conscious effort to shake off his depression. A drink would help.

They bought pints of lager and sat outside under the trees. On impulse, Tom told Roddy how disappointed they were that Lauren still wasn't pregnant. Roddy listened, nodded, sympathized, coughed, said, 'Yes, well, early days,' and seemed generally uneasy. Tom wondered why. Roddy was, after all, accustomed to conducting intimate conversations, but perhaps he didn't do it with friends? Then, suddenly, though nothing had been said, Tom knew why. Lauren must have told Angela he was impotent, and sometime later, in the aftermath perhaps of one of their unaesthetic but productive couplings, Angela had told Roddy.

After that, all he wanted to do was get away. He felt betrayed. Inevitably, though he told himself he had no right to blame Lauren. Why shouldn't she turn to her best friend for comfort? She got little enough from him. And he flayed himself, imagining Roddy and Angela giggling about it, knowing all the time they wouldn't have done, that they'd have been as sympathetic as he and Lauren would have been, if the roles had been reversed. But he knew, also, that next morning Roddy would have stood in the bathroom, contemplating his todger – must be years since he'd seen it without the aid of a mirror – feeling an unacknowledged flicker of amusement. So old Tom can't get it up? he would have thought. No, not even thought – would have permitted the thought into his mind only as a possible reaction, the hypothetical response of somebody altogether cruder and less compassionate than he was himself. Well, well, fancy that. And then he'd have toddled down to breakfast, whistling between his teeth in that irritating way of his, feeling more of a man because of it.

He had no right to blame Lauren for talking about their sexual difficulties, but he did. Somewhere in the back of his mind, as he and Roddy parted, was the picture of a rope, fraying, one strand after another coming apart.

FOUR

That evening, Tom read the report he'd written after
his visit to the remand centre to see Danny.

A dry, formal account of his assessment of the child.

Nothing in it about arriving early. Nothing about
the hot sunshine, or the prickly sweat on the backs of
his thighs, or the photographs, sliding out of a file
on the back seat. Nothing about the red-hot pokers
standing as witnesses to it all, eyeless and mute.

Nothing, either, about the shock of seeing Danny
come into the room. He knew he was a child, and yet
he was unprepared for the sight of the small boy
walking along the corridor and into the room beside
the warder. Because of his age, Danny had been asked
whether he wanted somebody else to be present: his
social worker, perhaps, or one of the warders, but
he'd said no, and so, after the warder withdrew and
closed the door behind him, they faced each other
alone.

Danny sat sideways in his chair, holding on to the

radiator behind him, an odd thing to do, Tom thought, in the heat, until he touched it himself and realized it was the coldest object in the room. The windows were high, made of frosted glass. Nobody could see either out or in. But when Tom suggested opening one of them, Danny, speaking for the first time, whispered, 'No. Somebody might hear.'

He took his hands off the radiator and covered his ears, pressing in and out. Tom's voice would be reaching him, if at all, as a muffled roar, masked by the whispering of his own blood. He screens out sounds, Tom thought. So sounds are important to him – voices are important. He made a conscious effort to speak gently, to ask simple questions. What did he prefer to be called? Did he like Daniel, or Danny, or Dan?

'Danny.'

'Have you got any pets, Danny?'

'A dog.'

'What's it called?'

'Duke.'

'What sort of dog is it?'

'A bull mastiff.'

'When you lived at home did you take him for walks?'

He shook his head.

'Why not?'

A shrug. 'Just didn't.'

The first ten minutes were spent like this.

'Have you got your own room?'

'Yes.'

'What's it like?'

'Okay.'

'What can you see out of the window?'

'A wall.'

'What sort of things do you do?'

A shrug.

'Do you have lessons?'

'Yes.'

'With the other boys?'

'No, just me.'

'What's that like?'

'Hard.'

'Why's it hard?'

'I've got to answer all the questions.'

Danny wasn't deceived. He knew the hard questions were coming, and that here too there would be nobody else to answer them.

'What do you do after lessons?'

'Watch telly.'

'What's your favourite programme?'

'Football.'

'Do you go outside?'

'Yes.'

'On your own?'

'No, with a warder.'

'Do you play with the other boys?'

'No.'

'Why not?'

'They're too big. They wouldn't want to play with me.'

'Would you like to play with them?'

'No.'

'Why not?'

At last, eye contact. A snarl of impatience. 'Because they'd kick me head in.'

'Why would they do that?'

Danny opened his mouth to tell Tom exactly why, then clamped it shut. He shrugged again, this time no more than a twitch of the shoulders. 'Because.'

He was a child. He lived in the present, and the present was dominated by his fear of the big boys. He was afraid that, one day, the warders would leave his door unlocked, and then the big boys would get him.

'But the warders won't do that, will they?'

'How do you know? They might.'

'They won't, Danny.'

He looked away, unconvinced.

'Is there anything else worrying you?'

He muttered something that Tom had to ask him to repeat.

'The trial.'

'What about the trial?'

'Everybody looking at me.'

'In the dock? But there'll be somebody with you. You won't be on your own.'

'Yes, I will.'

Those words, the fact that Danny didn't need to amplify them, and knew he didn't, marked a turning point. He took his hands away from his ears, leant forward, began to speak more freely. That day he talked endlessly about his father, how good he was at building things, how they used to go rabbiting together.

'But he doesn't live with you any more, does he?'

'No.'

'When did he leave? I mean, how long ago?'

'A year and . . .' He counted. 'Four months.'

'How did you feel about that?'

Nothing, not even a shrug. Danny didn't do feelings.

Over the next two hours, as Tom probed his emotional and moral maturity, his mental state, his fitness to stand trial in an adult court, Danny came out with some startling opinions. Startling in a child.

'Is it wrong to kill somebody?'

'Not always.'

'When is it all right?'

'If you're a soldier.'

'But if you're not a soldier, is it wrong?'

Danny shrugged. 'Thousands of people get killed all the time, all over the world. You know, people look at the telly, and they say, "Oh, isn't that awful?" But they don't mean it.'

'So people getting killed doesn't matter any more?'

'Not much.'

'What about Mrs Parks? Lizzie. Do you think it matters that she was killed?'

'I didn't kill her.'

'That's not what I asked.'

Danny took so long to answer that Tom began to think he never would. 'Yes,' he said, at last.

'A lot?'

'She was old.'

'So not a lot?'

Danny shook his head.

'I want to get this clear, Danny. You're saying it does matter that she's dead?'

'Yes.'

'But not very much, because she was old?'

'She'd had her life.'

For the first time he seemed to be quoting somebody else, though nobody would have said that to him about Lizzie. Tom sat back and took a moment to think. Immediately, Danny also sat back in his chair, a precise, almost synchronous mirroring of Tom's movement. Casually, Tom changed position again, this time resting his hands on the arms of his chair. Danny did the same. This was deliberate mimicry, not the unconscious echoing of the other person's posture that occurs in a conversation that's going well.

'You know when you used to go rabbiting with your dad. Did you ever kill a rabbit?'

'Yes.'

'Do you think it's different, killing a rabbit and killing a person?'

'Yes.'

'How is it different?'

Danny looked Tom full in the face. 'Rabbits run faster.'

He was an arrogant little bastard. 'But do you think people suffer more?' Silence. 'Somebody who was suffocated might suffer quite a bit.' Silence. 'Wouldn't they?' She, he wanted to say.

'Yes, but then they'd be dead.'

'So it wouldn't matter any more?'

'No, they'd be *dead*.'

'When people, or animals, die, do they stay dead?'

Danny looked at him as if he'd gone mad. ' 'Course they do. You wring a chicken's neck, you don't expect to find it running round the yard next morning, do you?'

Tom glanced down at his fingernails. 'So Lizzie can't come back?'

The question distressed Danny so much that for a while Tom thought he might have to suspend the interview. He held Danny's wrists, saying, 'C'mon, breathe. It's all right, Danny. Breathe.' At last, when he was relatively calm, Tom said, 'You can tell me, you know.'

Danny whispered, 'She does come back.'

'When?'

'Night-time.'

43

'You mean you dream about her?'

'No, she's there.'

'Is this just after you've woken up?'

'Yes.'

'What do you do about it?'

'There's nothing to do. I just look at her.'

'Do you try to stay awake?'

Yes, he made himself say the twelve times table backwards, and he put toy soldiers round his bed. 'I pretend they're my dad.'

'Do you ever see her during the day?'

'Yes.' A second later, 'But not the same.'

'What's it like during the day?'

'It sort of hits you. Like –' He brought both hands up to his face, as if he were going to hit himself in the eyes.

'What do you see?'

'Her.'

'What exactly?'

'Her. At the bottom of the stairs.'

Danny was pleading not guilty, so, in the course of the assessment, Tom could ask no questions about the murder. But Danny admitted being in Lizzie's house, shortly after the murder. His story was that he'd gone to see Lizzie because she'd told him one of her cats had had kittens and he wanted to see them. The backdoor was open, he thought she must have left it open for him, and so he'd gone in and found her lying dead at the foot of the stairs, the cushion that had been used to kill her lying over her face. He touched her – she was still warm – and lifted the cushion off her face, but put it back again immediately because she looked so horrible. And then he heard footsteps upstairs, realized the murderer must still be in the house, and ran for his life. He ran all the way home, and hid in the barn. He didn't tell anybody because he was afraid the man would come and kill him if he did.

None of this was true. The forensic evidence for Danny's guilt was overwhelming, but he was a good liar.

'So the hairs on your jumper were Lizzie's?'

'They were *white*. I haven't suddenly turned into an old man, have I?'

Tom waited, then said, 'Must feel a bit like it, sometimes.'

Danny said nothing. Just wrapped his arms round himself, and hugged his narrow chest.

There were things Danny wouldn't talk about. He wouldn't talk at all about his mother. At one point, Tom tried using dolls to get him to speak more freely, but Danny was so uncomfortable playing with them that the attempt had to be abandoned. He had no more idea at the end of the interview than he'd had at the beginning what forces in Danny's background could have led him to commit such a crime.

On the other hand, a clear picture of Danny's present mental state did emerge. He was sleeping badly, he had nightmares, he suffered flashbacks, he couldn't concentrate, he felt numb, he complained that everything around him seemed unreal. But none of these symptoms was any guide to his state of mind at the time of the killing.

Towards the end of the three hours, Tom asked Danny about his fire-setting. Why did he light fires?

'For a laugh. Everybody does it.'

'*Everybody* sets fire to their bedroom?'

Silence. Tom got a box of matches out of his pocket and pushed them across the table to Danny, who tucked his hands more firmly into his armpits.

'Go on,' Tom said, 'light one.'

Slowly Danny reached for the box, his hand creeping across the table like a small animal. A rasp and flare as he struck the match. A doubled reflection of the flame appeared in his eyes, whose pupils had not contracted, as one would have expected, but grown large, as if starved of light.

'Blow it out when you're ready.'

Danny swallowed. The flame licked the wood.

'Danny . . .'

He didn't move. Tom leant forward and blew. An acrid smell, a coil of blue smoke hanging in the air like a question mark.

'Must have hurt.'

Danny shook his head.

'Let's see.'

Slowly, the small fist uncurled, revealing fingertips smooth and shiny where the skin had burnt. Danny was staring at him, and Tom had no idea whether this was a deliberate act of defiance, or whether he loved fire so much that he'd been incapable of blowing the match out.

When Tom judged Danny had had enough, he summoned the warder. Danny looked startled, as if the end of the interview came as an unpleasant shock. Tom held out his hand, as he always did after the opening session with a child, but, instead of shaking hands, Danny threw himself into Tom's arms. For a moment, Tom didn't move, but it wasn't in him to reject such a gesture from a child in trouble, and he returned the hug. 'C'mon, Danny. Don't cry, it'll be all right.' Though he knew it wouldn't, and Danny had more reason than most to cry.

'By heck,' the warder said, as they were walking down the corridor together. 'You must have a strong stomach.' Seeing Tom's expression change, he added defensively, 'Well, he is a horror, isn't he?'

It was so common for loving mothers to describe their children as 'little horrors' that it was startling to hear the word used in that precise, almost archaic sense. As soon as he got home, Tom looked it up.

In pencil, in the margin of his notes, he'd jotted the definition down:

1 (A painful feeling of) intense loathing or fear; a terrified and revolted shuddering; a strong aversion or an intense dislike (*of*); *colloq.* dismay (*at*) 2 The

47

quality of exciting intense loathing and fear; a person who or thing which excites such feelings; *colloq.* a mischievous person, esp. a child.

In Tom's view there was no point in thinking about Danny, or any other child, in such terms. His job was simply to decide on the degree of Danny's mental and moral maturity. There were huge gaps in his information − he had no clear picture of Danny's family, for example − but he thought he had enough to answer the main questions. Could Danny distinguish between fantasy and reality? Did he understand that killing was wrong? Did he understand that death is a permanent state? Was he, in short, capable of standing trial, on a charge of murder, in an adult court? And to all these questions Tom had answered, Yes. Not without doubt, not without qualification, not without many hours of soul searching, but, in the end, *Yes*.

FIVE

Tom went to bed late, expecting a bad night, but in fact he fell into a deep sleep almost immediately. Towards dawn he woke, lay for a few moments, dazed, in the half-light, then drifted off again, and dreamt about his father. He was in a crowded pub, edging between the tables with pint glasses in his hand, when he looked down and saw broad shoulders in a herringbone tweed jacket, the back of a curly, grizzled head. 'Dad?' he said. The man looked up. It was his father, though with dream logic he had to look at the missing tip of the middle finger on his right hand before he could be sure.

The dream changed. Now they were walking down a street with a high wall on their left. The joy and relief of being able to talk to him again. Then something started to go wrong. 'I have to go now,' Dad said. 'My rabbit's gone wonky.' And he shrank, not slowly, but catastrophically, like a balloon when the air's let out, and became a bit of rag, a scrap of paper, something flying above Tom's head, over the wall and out of sight. Tom grabbed the top of the wall and scrabbled up. He was looking into an old churchyard, headstones almost hidden by tall grass, and a rabbit running between the graves. A voice said, 'That's what a great love comes to – a rabbit running between graves.'

Hearing the voice, Tom realized he was awake, though it took several more minutes for him to realize that the voice was part of the dream. It had moved him deeply. The joy of being with his father, and the sadness of losing him again, remained with him and coloured the day.

'When are you coming home?' his mother had asked, though the bungalow she lived in now had never been his home. Not that half-mythical place where dead leaves under a rhododendron bush brought back the time when he was two years old, small enough to crawl under the bush and believe himself forgotten, while adult feet, his mother's in sandals, his father's in the cracked, brown shoes he wore for gardening, tramped to and fro, and adult voices, loud, artificial, asked, 'Where's Tom? Have you seen Tom? I can't think where he's got to, can you?' And he'd giggled nervously, afraid he might really be lost, invisible, relieved when his father pounced on him, shouting through the shiny green leaves, 'I've got him! Here he is!'

They'd moved into the bungalow a year before his father's death, when it became clear that the wheel-chair he persisted in treating as a temporary inconvenience was going to be nothing of the kind. It was on the outskirts of a small country town, only five minutes' drive from the motorway interchange. 'We can be anywhere,' his mother had said proudly, 'in half an hour.' Though she'd gone nowhere while his father was alive. The local shops, hurrying there and back, had been the limit of her range.

He set off early. As he dropped down into the Vale of York, a thin mist began to drift across the road, clotting in the hollows, reducing him to a walking pace. Cows, white vapour draped around their horns, came to the fence and chewed as the car crawled past. Then, as quickly as it had come, the mist cleared, and the sun shone. It looked like being a hot day.

He passed the pub where he and his father had gone for what turned out to be their last drink together, though they hadn't walked, as in the dream: he'd pushed his father there, horrifically used to doing it by then. His father sat hunched forward, dissociating himself from the chair. He only consented to be seen in it at all because in this village he was relatively unknown. He, who in his irascible way had preached patience to patients for years, never got used to the effects of his stroke, never accepted the damage, always turned his face away, even from those closest to him, to hide the disfiguring sneer. He wouldn't adjust, wouldn't accept that the changes were permanent, and he was right there, though death, not recovery, returned the wheelchair to the garage. Where it still was. Not because of any sentimental attachment, but because nobody had yet summoned up the energy to give it away.

He slowed and turned right into the drive, and Tyger, his mother's cat, came slowly across the lawn to greet him, white-tipped tail held aloft, rubbing his face against Tom's ankle almost before he was out of the car. 'Hello, there,' he said, bending down to rub the backs of Tyger's ears.

His mother must have been waiting for the car. He saw her, blurred and tenuous through frosted glass, before he had time to press the bell. Opening the door, she started to cry, then stopped herself. He kissed her, and felt the scrumpled tissue of her cheek too soft against his lips. He didn't like the way her flesh was sagging, knew it was too fast, that she was losing weight, probably neglecting herself, but he didn't know what to do about it, or how to raise the topic without appearing to nag.

'How are you, Mum?'

'Not so bad.'

It was always 'not so bad'. He fully expected to hear those words from inside her coffin. Because of the heat – the bungalow's picture windows turned any warm day into a scorcher – she was wearing a short-sleeved white t-shirt, and he saw how the flesh on her arms hung loose from the bone. She was still only sixty-two, but some people wither quickly in the absence of physical love, and he knew instinctively how good his parents' love-making had been. It was one of the reasons why, as a teenager, he'd felt different from other kids. They thought of their parents as 'past it' – he knew he hadn't reached it. (Still hadn't, for that matter, and time was running out.)

'I thought we'd just have a salad,' she was saying. 'It's a bit warm, isn't it, for anything hot?'

He poured her the first of the two sherries she allowed herself before lunch, and himself a strong gin and tonic. They took their glasses out to the patio. Tyger jumped on to the table, squeezing his golden eyes shut several times in token of friendship, before losing interest in the proceedings altogether and going to sleep.

The garden stretched out, not so much in front of them, as above them, for Tom's father, in the last year of his life, had supervised the building of raised flower beds, beds he could reach from the wheelchair he refused to admit was permanent. 'It'll be easier for your mother's back,' he'd told Tom unblushingly, though then she'd suffered no more than the usual slight creaks of middle age.

Now her arthritis was so bad, his mother was saying, the raised beds were a godsend. She got up, face tense with what she always referred to as 'discomfort', and showed him, with the trowel that lay always ready to hand, how easy it was for her to turn the soil. Then, heavily, back to the chair, his father's evasion turned into reality, and Tom found himself wondering how deep loyalty can go.

It was mid September. The late roses were still at their best; her arms were scored with red scratches where the gloves didn't reach. He knew she was dreading the winter, when there would be nothing, or little, to do, except on the afternoons she worked at the Community Centre.

A year ago she'd been gearing herself up to face retirement. 'You'll keep busy,' he'd said. 'I bet six months after you retire you'll be wondering how to fit everything in.' He'd meant, You're used to coping with loss. You're good at it. Now he looked at her and wondered whether she was coping at all.

On the way over he'd been wondering whether to tell her about the dream he'd had about his father, and had almost decided not to, but sitting there, looking at the garden his father had started to make, and not lived to complete, he did tell her. It was one of their rules that his father's name should be frequently on their lips, not obsessively, but casually, naturally, as absent friends are mentioned. But when he came to the ludicrous conclusion: that's what a great love comes to, a rabbit running between graves, he hadn't the heart to repeat it.

'What an extraordinary dream,' she said when he'd

finished, and then, with barely a pause, 'Of course the rabbits *are* a problem.'

Tom felt himself go cold, a light chill, as if a cloud had drifted over the sun, but then realized she'd gone back to talking about the garden. Rabbits, from the gorse-covered hills behind the bungalow, regularly ate her new plants. You saw their bright, round, shiny pellets in clusters all over the lawn.

This October would be the second anniversary of his father's death. Some textbooks describe grieving for more than six months as prolonged. They were well into injury time, though they'd grieved like professionals: brought the body home, kept the coffin open, visited him frequently, in the cold room, with the windows wide open and a single light burning by his head. They'd touched his hands, become familiar with the density of dead flesh, watched the minute changes of expression as the rigor mortis wore off. And yet none of this had been enough to make them accept the reality of his going. He had been, even in his final illness, too large a presence. She still heard the hiss of wheelchair tyres along the wet paths, his voice calling for her from another room, because he'd depended on her totally in that last illness, not merely for the physical needs of life, but for her presence, her touch, her voice, her smell. As the sexual bond loosened, it had been replaced by this other, maternal, bond, equally physical, so that for her there had been no release from the white heat of bodily closeness in which their lives had been lived. It was too great a gap to be filled.

But they persevered. They got the photograph album out as soon as they could bear to, and laughed and cried over old memories, guiding themselves gently past the last photographs of him in the chair, reminiscing about family holidays, the dogs they'd kept when Tom was a child.

A year after his father's death she still, occasionally, laid the table for two.

On the first anniversary she went to the local RSPCA refuge and adopted Tyger, a three-year-old tabby whose previous owner had died. The owner's other four cats had been rehomed without difficulty, but Tyger grieved ceaselessly, irreconcilably, turning his back – literally – on anybody who tried to make friends. In the end he'd been placed in a carer's home, where he took up residence inside a doll's house, glaring through its latticed windows, coming out only to eat and use his tray. 'That's the one,' his mother said. 'Come on, Tyger. Let's go and be miserable together.' Stage four of grieving: the transference of libido to another object, person or activity. Tom's mother made more rapid progress with this than Tyger, who, for the first three months, retreated behind the sofa, and spat.

The natural love object, the one that would have contributed enormously to her recovery, was a grand-child, but that he was, rather conspicuously, failing to supply.

'How's Lauren?' she asked.

'Fine. Fine. She seems to be enjoying herself.'

'Coming home this weekend?'

'No, she's going to see her parents. It's their fortieth wedding anniversary soon, so they're all planning the party.'

'You should go with her, Tom.'

'I'm not invited.'

'Oh.' She swished her drink round the bottom of the glass, not looking at him. 'It's not good, is it?'

'Everybody has bad patches, Mum.'

She nodded her acceptance. 'Come on, let's eat.'

The meal passed in gentle, inconsequential chat. Jeff Bridges, his best friend from primary-school days, was getting a divorce. 'He was always trouble, that one,' Tom's mother said, rather harshly he thought. Marriage wasn't easy, and Jeff had embarked on it far too young. Home from university for the first long vacation, he'd met Jeff pushing his eldest daughter in her pram. Tom had felt like a schoolboy, still, in comparison with Jeff, though he'd had sense enough not to envy him.

Just as they were finishing lunch, a sudden squall of rain blew up. Shadows of black clouds, chasing each other up the hill, dowsed the gorse. Tom dashed out to lower the parasol, wrestling with its damp folds, feeling drops of rain patter on to his back through the thin shirt. The slap of wet cloth against his face exhilarated him, and he went back into the house, glowing.

As soon as they finished their coffee, he said, 'I think I should be getting back.'

They embraced on the doorstep, but his mother was the one who broke the embrace first. A scrupulously honourable woman, she would never, for a second, leech off her son's life, or use him in any way as a substitute for his father. 'Ring when you get back,' was all she said.

Danny Miller had been at the back of his mind all day, and he wanted, before setting off home, to revisit a place he had played in as a child. It was only a few miles away, a slight detour off the main road. He pulled on to the grass verge, and set off to walk the rest of the way.

The path to the pond seemed less clear, less well trodden, than when he was a boy, and he and Jeff Bridges came here to play. The recent heavy rain had turned dips into quagmires. He edged past them, shuffling sideways along the steep verge, hawthorn twigs snagging on his shirt. Pushing down the green tunnel, he seemed to be going back into the past. He wouldn't have been surprised to meet his ten-year-old self coming in the other direction, holding a jam jar, the murky water thick with tiddlers or tadpoles. Or spawn.

They'd been looking for spawn that day. He and Jeff had wanted to go off by themselves, but instead they'd been saddled with Neil, the four-year-old son of some friends of Jeff's parents who'd turned up for the weekend and wanted to go for a drink in a pub that didn't take children. 'The boys can play together,' Jeff's father had said easily, ignoring Jeff's muttered, 'Da-ad, do we have to?'

They were told to stay in the garden. They did, for about twenty minutes, playing piggy in the middle. Neil had to be the piggy because he couldn't throw the ball. They sent it high above his head, getting a sour pleasure from his increasing bewilderment as he ran to and fro. Then, bored, they decided on a quick visit to the pond, got their jam jars and set off, dragging Neil after them. He was a polite, solemn little boy, with dark-rimmed glasses and an anxious expression. Grown-ups thought Neil was cute, kids thought he came from another planet. He trotted along with his mouth open, breathing noisily through his nose because he'd been told not to breathe through his mouth, and Neil always did what he was told. 'We're going to get frog spawn, Neil,' Jeff said, in the spuriously excited, isn't-this-fun tone of voice he'd heard used by adults (mainly adults who didn't like children very much).

Wellies, that day. It wasn't raining, but in spring all the paths were deep in mud. Once they'd got to the pond they saw that the frog spawn – newly laid, standing proud above the water – was five or six feet away from the bank. Too deep for wellies, so they pulled them off and stood on the edge of the pond, barefoot, cold goose shit oozing up between their toes. Neil prattled away, poking at the sandy bank with a stick, ignored by both of them.

The pond was on a farmer's land, though not visible from the farmhouse. You weren't supposed to play there, because the pond wasn't a proper pond at all, but a flooded well. Out there, in the clear centre, where no weeds grew, there was a drop of a hundred feet.

Thirty years later, standing on the edge of the same pond, Tom wondered if that were true. It sounded like the kind of story adults might tell to frighten the children away, but he couldn't be sure. They'd waded out up to their waists once, daring each other to go further, but then Jeff stubbed his toe on a stone, and, panicking, they'd splashed back into the shallows. Behind the fringe of willow trees on the far bank was a road, quiet, since the building of the bypass five years ago, but then, busy, cars, buses and lorries roaring past.

No geese today. Then, they'd honked and hissed and swayed off, to stand at a slight distance, malevolent and watchful, as Tom started to wade into the pond. His feet raised clouds of fine mud. Frogs kicked away into the weeds, tiny males clinging to the fat females, even in the emergency of this invasion unable to let go. They dived into the mud and reappeared further out, croaking mournfully, their eyes like blackcurrants breaking the surface.

New spawn, the jelly still firm with tadpoles like full stops. Old spawn, slack jelly, tadpoles like commas. Tom lowered the jam jar beneath the surface, easing mounds of silvery slobber over the rim. Some of it was too firm to flow; he had to pull it apart to get it in. When he'd got enough, he turned round and saw Jeff, scooping spawn into his own jar, and behind him, wobbling precariously, still wearing his wellies, Neil.

It started as a joke. A cruel joke, yes, but still a joke. Whose idea was it to put frog spawn into Neil's wellies? He couldn't remember. Jeff's, he thought, but then he needed to think that.

Neil screamed as the heavy jelly slopped over the tops of his boots and filled them to the brim, pressing in on his bare legs. He wasn't hurt, he just couldn't bear the cold slime on his skin. He screamed and screamed, jumped up and down, fell over, got up again, soaked, face smeared with snot, piss coursing down his legs. There was no way out. The more he screamed, the more they panicked. They couldn't take him home like this, and they couldn't clean him up. Jeff scrambled on to the bank, Tom followed, but Neil couldn't move. They shouted at him to get out, but when he tried to move the spawn shifted and squelched inside his wellies, and he screamed again.

Jeff threw the first stone. Tom was sure about that. Almost sure. Little stones, pebbles, plopping into the water around the screaming child, who backed further out towards the centre of the pond. Why did they do it? Because they were frightened, because they shouldn't have been there at all, because they knew they were going to get into trouble, because they hated him, because he was a problem they couldn't solve, because neither could be the first to back down. Bigger clods of earth landed in the pond, not too close, they weren't trying to hit him yet. The frogs submerged and did not reappear. The geese retreated, honking and swaying, as they made their way up the hill.

And then a bus came past. A man, glancing up from his paper, peered through the window, hardly able to credit what he saw, and immediately jumped up and rang the bell. The driver, who could have decided to be awkward, stopped the bus, and minutes later the man – Tom never knew his name – careered down the bank, waded into the pond up to his knees, and gathered Neil into his arms. He carried him all the way home, having got the address out of a subdued and frightened Jeff. They followed him, stomping along behind, too shocked to speak, leaving the jam jars marooned in muddy footprints by the side of the pond.

Three children were saved that day. A man glances up from his newspaper, sees what's going on, acts on what he sees. Accident. A more interesting news story, a thicker coat of dirt on the bus window, a disinclination to intervene, and it might have ended differently.

In tragedy, perhaps. It might have. He didn't know. It was his good fortune not to know.

Had he known at the time that what he was doing was wrong? Yes, undoubtedly. His parents had been easy, tolerant, in many ways, but in all essential matters the moral teaching had been firm and clear. Cruelty to animals, deliberate unkindness, bullying smaller children: these were major crimes. What interested him was how little sense of responsibility he felt now. If somebody had asked him about that afternoon, he'd have said something like, 'Kids can be very cruel.' Not, 'I was very cruel.' 'Kids can be very cruel.' He knew he'd done it, he remembered it clearly, he'd known then, and accepted now, that it was wrong, but the sense of moral responsibility was missing. In spite of the connecting thread of memory, the person who'd done that was not sufficiently like his present self for him to feel guilt.

It was something to be borne in mind, he thought, strolling back to his car, in talking to Danny.

SIX

He was watching the Channel 4 news when the doorbell rang. Looking through the peephole, he saw
Danny, trapped in the distorting glass, like a fish in a
bowl. 'Hello, you're early,' Tom said, holding the
door open.

Danny stepped across the threshold, his shadow,
thrown by the porch light, leaping ahead of him as if
it already knew the way. 'I didn't know how long it
would take.'

'Never mind. Come in.'.

Tom took Danny's coat and hung it up.

'Can I get you a drink?'

'What are you having?'

'Whisky.'

'That'll do fine.'

Tom was remembering the other room, the one in
which they'd first met. The shock of seeing the small
boy walk in beside the warder. Now he was experi-
encing a similar shock. Danny's height, the depth of

his voice, the hunched power of his shoulders, the stillness – all these perfectly ordinary characteristics seemed bizarre, so powerfully did Tom sense the presence of that child, immured inside the man.

What was back, without effort, without his wanting it even, was the intimacy of that first meeting.

'Well, how have you been?' he asked, settling into an armchair.

'Since I left hospital? Tired. I went to bed and slept for ten hours. Woke up, didn't know where I was.'

Not an easy situation, this, Tom thought. You could hardly pretend it was a social call, and yet it wasn't a consultation either. He was going to have to feel his way forward. 'Do you want to talk about it?'

A shrug, bringing memories of their first meeting flooding back. 'Don't mind.'

'Quite a decision at your age. How old are you?'

'You know how old I am.' A pause. 'Twenty-three.'

'So what went wrong? After you came out?'

A faint smile. 'I met a girl. I was living with a Quaker couple at the time, and they're very nice but also quite elderly and a bit strait-laced, and I decided I'd rather live with the girl. It wasn't a great big thing.' He dropped his voice into the bass register. '*We are now committing ourselves to each other*. We were students, students live together. But Mike – the probation officer I had then – told me I had to tell her, and if I didn't tell her, he'd tell her. So of course I broke it off. I didn't dare risk it.'

'Did she mean a lot to you?'

Danny pursed his lips. 'Dunno. She was nice. Is nice. I don't suppose it was . . . You know, some of it was just me proving I could do it with a girl. I mean the bulk of my experience . . . Uh, the bulk, he says. 99.9 per cent of my experience has been the other sort.' A gulp of whisky. 'Not all of it voluntary. It's the one thing – '

'No, go on.'

'I was going to say it's the one thing I'm bitter about, but then I've got no right to be bitter about anything. Have I?'

In the courtroom, Tom had seen Danny smile at his social worker, and thought, Don't smile. Don't laugh, don't look pleased or excited, don't fidget, don't scratch your bum, don't pick your nose, or wriggle, or do any of the things kids do all the time. Not now, not ever. 'If that's what you feel . . .'

'Yeah, well, okay, I feel bitter. I think they should just come right out with it, you know? "I sentence you to be raped. By some big ugly bastard who's built like a brick shithouse, uses his arm as a pincushion, and isn't wearing a condom."'

'You don't mean, you're – '

'Oh no. Got lucky there. I'm just naturally slim.'

Danny crossed his legs at the ankle, a conscious display that made Tom want to smile. Wasted on me, son, he thought. Though he could see it wouldn't be wasted on everybody.

Rape was too intimate a revelation for the first ten minutes of a meeting. Either Danny had no sense of normal social distance and pacing (and where would Danny have acquired that?) or he too had a sense of falling through a trapdoor in the present, into the closeness of their first meeting. Tom kept using words like 'intimacy' and 'closeness' to describe the atmosphere of that meeting, but there'd also been massive antagonism. As there was now. And yet Danny had trusted him then, he thought, looking into the adult Danny's amused and trustless eyes. 'Anyway, the relationship broke up?' he said.

'Yes. And then I was told I couldn't teach.'

'Why not?'

'Not allowed to work with children. Actually, not allowed to work with people.'

Tom said gently, 'But you can see the point, can't you? I mean if you were a parent and you found out your child's teacher had been convicted of murder, how would you feel?'

'I hope I'd think it was a long time ago.'

'Would you?'

A silent struggle. 'No, probably not. But it threw me, you see, because I'm just starting the third year – I did three years of an Open University degree, inside, when I was in prison, and you can transfer the credits – and I thought teaching was what I'm going to do, and now I don't know *what* I'm going to do. And, you know, the whole thing pisses me off, because last year, I was released in November and I couldn't get a job, so I decided I'd be a gardener, only there wasn't any work so I thought I'd be a tree surgeon. I was turning up at old people's houses with a chainsaw, asking them if there was anything they wanted lopping off. Nobody worried about that.'

'Did you tell – Mike, was it? The probation officer? – about the chainsaw?'

'No.'

'Might be why he wasn't worried.'

Danny smiled. 'The point is, he had no need to be.'

'But they have to be ultra-careful, don't they? And so do you. One silly little incident, and you're back inside.'

'No, it's not that. You see the real question is: can people change?' Danny was leaning forward, meeting Tom's gaze with an almost uncomfortable intensity. 'And all sorts of people whose jobs actually depend on a belief that people can change, social workers, probation officers, clinical psychologists' – he smiled – 'psychiatrists, don't really believe it at all.'

'Well, yes – because those are precisely the jobs that furnish people with a good deal of evidence that it doesn't happen.'

'Do you believe it?'

Tom leant back, massaging the skin of his forehead, his face partially screened from Danny's gaze. 'It would be very easy for me to say yes, but I suspect in the sense you mean, I . . . don't. Obviously, if you take a particular individual and change his environment, completely, for a long time, he's going to learn new tricks. He's got to, the old tricks don't work any more, and he's an organism that's programmed to survive. If he's capable of learning at all, he'll learn. My God, he will. But I don't think the responses are genuinely new, I think they were there all along. Lying dormant. Because they weren't needed.'

'So the logic is, if you put this "particular individual" back into the old situation, with all the old pressures, he'll revert to the old responses.'

'The old situation might not still be there.'

'But if it was? He'd revert?'

'Not necessarily. There's always the hope that some of the new tricks might carry over.'

'But he might revert?'

'Yes. There's always that possibility.'

Danny crossed his arms and leant back in his chair. 'You're a cynical sod, really, aren't you? Under all that compassion you don't actually give a toss for anybody.'

'Whereas you believe in redemption.'

Danny was so startled his nostrils flared. 'Oooooh,' he said, midway between a sigh and a groan. 'I don't know that I do. I'd like to.' He paused. 'Of course in your terms that would be a genuinely new response.'

'Yes.'

A short silence. Danny said, 'Sorry.'

'What for?'

'Calling you a cynical sod.'

'That's all right, you don't have to be polite.'

He didn't. This was now definitely not a social call. 'Tell me about going back to prison.'

'Nothing much to tell. It was . . . impulse, really. I just thought, Sod it, I can't make it work. And in a curious sort of way, I did make prison work, I'd got a job in the library, I was doing a degree.' His expression hardened. 'And I could work with people. If somebody wanted to talk, they talked. They knew bloody well I wasn't going to pass it on.'

'So you had a role?'

'Yeah, which is more than I've bloody well got out here. So I went back. Hitched most of the way, walked the last ten miles. And then I bumped into one of the warders, one of the better ones, and he said, "Come and have a cup of tea." And I told him what I was doing and he said, "Don't be daft, Danny, they're not going to let you back in." And that was the first time anybody had called me Danny for months, so that didn't discourage me. Anyway I banged on the door and I've no doubt he'd rung ahead and warned them I was coming. I was put in the visitors' waiting room. There was this girl there with a baby, visiting somebody, she thought I was visiting too. And then Martha came and got me. Stupid.'

'It was understandable.'

'Gerraway, man. It was pathetic.'

A sudden incursion of a Geordie accent. Why? 'How long ago was that?'

'Nine days.'

'Is that what made you so depressed?'

'No, I'd been feeling down for months. It's always bad in the vacations when everybody else goes home.'

'Can't you go home?'

'My mother's dead.'

'Oh, I am sorry.' Tom remembered her clearly, a woman with mousy fair hair, wearing a blue cardigan that matched the faded blue of her eyes. In the course of the trial, her eyes seemed to become paler, as if tears could dilute the colour. She'd wept, quietly, persistently, into an embroidered handkerchief, the sort almost nobody carried any more, and Tom had been conscious of mounting irritation as the furtive sniffling went on and on. You'd have thought she was the victim. Danny looked round at her continually, more worried about her, it seemed, than he was about himself. And even that had counted against him, making him seem mature beyond his years. 'When did it happen?'

'Two years ago. Of course I was still inside. They took me to see her in the hospital, only they wouldn't take the handcuffs off, so she had all the shame of other people, nurses, seeing me like that. And we couldn't talk, with the warder there. And then she got a lot worse, and I asked if I could go to see her again, and the governor hummed and hawed and . . . finally said yes. And I stood to attention, and said, "Thank you, sir." I should've ripped his fucking liver out.'

Tom let a silence open up. Then he said, 'I hope you're careful who you say that to.'

A direct gaze. 'I am. At the funeral I was in handcuffs again – of course. When I bent down to throw earth on the coffin, I had to kind of coordinate it with the warder, like a bloody three-legged race. It was ridiculous.'

'So there's no home base?'

'No.'

'What about your father?'

'Haven't seen him for years. He used to come and see me at Long Garth. You know, it was almost like a posh school, sort of place he went to. I think he quite liked that, so long as he didn't have to remember why I was there.' He stopped, patted his pockets. 'Do you mind if I smoke?'

'No, go ahead.'

He used matches still. Tom put an ashtray near him and went back to his chair.

'I did try to talk to him once.'

'About?'

'The obvious. He got up and walked out. I can't remember if that was the last visit. If it wasn't, there weren't many more.'

'What about last Saturday?'

'I woke up feeling quite good, actually. I'd got the second anniversary of my mother's death over, and I thought, Right now, for Christ's sake, start moving on. And then . . . I don't know what happened. I just fell into the pit. I was wandering round, I'd had quite a bit to drink – that didn't help – and I was near the river, and I thought, Sod it.'

'Like when you went back to prison?'

'It was a bit like that, yes. Except worse, because then I knew there wasn't anywhere to go.'

'So you didn't plan it at all?'

'No.'

Danny's face was veiled in smoke. Not that it mattered. Any good liar – and Danny was exceptionally good – can control his expression. It's the body that gives the game away. Tom thought he could discern a new tension in Danny's posture, a choppiness in the movement of the hands. When he said 'No', he'd tried to shrug, but only one shoulder moved. And who carries temazepam around with them in the middle of the day? No, Danny was telling, at best, a partial truth.

'I'm glad it happened,' Danny said.

'Why?'

'Because I met you. Again. And I know you're going to laugh, but I still think that wasn't an accident.'

You and me both, Tom thought. 'So what was it, then?'

'It was, I dunno, a sort of kick in the pants, I suppose, because I'd tried to go on ignoring it and pretending it didn't happen and suddenly there it is, bang. Right in front of me.'

'And that's a sign you have to face up to it?'

'Yes.'

'You're putting an awful lot on coincidence, Danny. I mean, you get fished out of the river by a psychologist, so you decide it's time for some psychotherapy. Suppose I'd been a tailor. Would you have ordered a suit?'

'That's not fair. And it's not *a* psychologist, is it?'

Tom took time to think. 'You know, if you're really serious about this, there's quite a strong argument for starting at the beginning with somebody else.'

'No. It's you or nobody. And by the way, I don't want psychotherapy. Why would I want that? I want to work out why it happened.' He waited. 'It's not as if we had a personal relationship.'

'No, that's true. Did you ever get any treatment?'

'No. Don't look so shocked. You were the one who told the court I was normal.'

'I didn't say you were normal. I said you were suffering from post-traumatic stress disorder.'

'Yeah, well, they forgot about that. Look, it was made pretty clear you didn't talk about it. Not to anybody. Mr Greene, that was the headmaster at Long Garth, actually said, on the first night, I don't care what you've done. Nobody's going to ask you about that. This is the first day of the rest of your life. And everybody did what he said. There was an English teacher there, and I wrote something for him, but not about the murder. I couldn't talk to my mother.

Floods of tears the minute she walked through the door. And when I tried to talk to my father –'

'He got up and walked out.'

'Yes.'

A long pause. Danny was looking down at his hands. Nails neatly manicured, cuticles picked raw. Tom waited.

'When my mother died,' Danny said at last, 'somebody sent me some photographs, and there was one of me as a little boy, pushing one of those trolley things, you know, with bricks inside. I'd have been about two, I suppose. And I look at that photograph, and – I look like a normal little kid. I know, you can say, "Well, what do you expect? Horns?" But that's it, you see. I just want to know why.'

'Danny, if we're going to do this . . .' Tom raised both hands. 'And I'm not saying we are. I think you have to think very carefully about whether . . . about whether you're up to it. Because it's not a simple matter of getting the facts straight. It's . . . you're going to be dredging up the emotions as well. Do you see that?'

'Yes. Yes.'

'No, not "Yes, yes." *Think*. If you start this, and then you have to stop because it's too painful, you're going to feel you've failed. And if you do manage to go on, there're going to be times when you feel a lot worse than you do at the moment. And what I've got to remember is that a couple of days ago you tried to kill yourself.'

'But I'm not depressed.' Danny waited for a reply. 'Do *you* think I'm depressed?'

Tom hesitated. 'I see no sign of it.' What he couldn't say was that he didn't find the absence of depressive symptoms reassuring.

'Well, then. What you . . . sorry, what I don't seem to be able to get across is that I don't want therapy. I don't want to "feel better". I simply want to know what happened and why.'

Tom took a moment to think. 'Danny, a lot of people would say the real priority for you is to tackle the problems you've got now. You can't change the past, but you can change the present.'

A wintry smile. 'It's up to me to set my priorities.'

'Yes, that's true.'

Danny leant forward. 'Can I ask you what you think – no, sorry what you *feel* – about the trial?'

'What I feel? I'm not sure my feelings are relevant.'

'Oh, I think they are.'

Tom's mind flooded with images of the courtroom. The small, lonely figure in the dock. 'Uneasy,' he said at last.

Danny smiled. 'You see? That's what I mean. You want it to be doctor and patient, or expert witness and accused. But it . . . it isn't just that *I* don't want it to be like that . . . it *isn't* like that.'

'We seem to be making sense of the trial now, Danny. I thought it was the murder you wanted to talk about.'

'It's not much of a choice, is it? One led to the other. You see, all this stuff about, Can I can stand it? Is it going to make me worse? Shouldn't I be thinking about sorting out the problems I've got now? It's all a load of . . .' Another unexpectedly charming smile. 'With respect, bollocks. Because in the end you need this as much as I do.'

Tom sat back in his chair, arms folded across his chest, not caring about the body language, wanting every bone and muscle to express what he felt. 'Danny,' he said, 'if you have the slightest suspicion that I need . . . anything out of this, you should run a mile.'

'I'm sorry. I need this very badly, and I don't . . . I don't know how to put this. I don't always manage to distinguish between what I'm feeling and what other people are feeling. I seem to be –'

'Permeable?'

A short laugh of recognition. 'Yes, I suppose. More than most people.'

That was an impressive display of self-knowledge, Tom thought. 'Look, let's leave it for now. I need to talk to Martha, and of course you do realize there's no question of going ahead if she doesn't agree? And even if she does agree, I still haven't made up my mind.'

'All right,' Danny said, putting his glass on the table. 'I haven't handled this very well, have I?'

'Oh, I don't think you did too badly.'

SEVEN

Martha Pitt called first thing next morning, her smoke-roughened voice sounding, as it always did on the phone, slightly tentative. It had taken him a long time to work out why. It wasn't that she disliked the phone; she just hated giving her name. At first he'd thought it was her nickname – 'Pit Bull Martha' – that she disliked, and you could see why – not a lot of women would have liked it – but it turned out to be 'Martha' she couldn't stand. 'How do you think it feels? Condemned from the cradle to choose the worser part.'

'What is the worser part?'

'Doing good, rather than contemplating God.'

Martha was a Catholic. She knew that sort of thing.

'Bloody good name for a probation officer, then.'

'Aw, piss off.'

Now she said crisply, 'I think we need to talk.'

'What about?' he asked, teasing.

'Ian Wilkinson.'

They arranged to meet for lunch at one o'clock. He'd been standing at the bar for five minutes when Martha came in, clutching the enormous black satchel she carted around with her everywhere. Sometimes, watching her scrabble about inside it for something she knew she had somewhere, he imagined her disappearing into it, backwards, dragging make-up, car keys, court reports in after her, like a badger pulling fresh bedding into its sett.

Bending to kiss her, he breathed in the familiar smells of stale cigarette smoke and peppermints. She'd become addicted to mints during her last attempt to give up smoking, and now scoured sweetshops for stronger and stronger varieties. Fiery Fred was her latest fix. The last time they'd met he'd made the mistake of accepting one, and his eyes had watered for a full five minutes afterwards.

'Do you want a pint?' he asked.

He waited, patiently, while the usual struggle with temptation played itself out on her features, ending as it always did. 'Yeah, go on, why not?'

'Cheers,' Tom said, raising his glass. 'Probably the end of useful work for the day, but never mind.'

'How's it going?'

'Not bad. I ought to finish the first draft by the end of next week.'

'Then I can start reading?'

'Yes. Gently.'

They took their glasses over to a table by the

window and sat down. 'Well, then,' Martha said, lighting a cigarette, 'how does it feel to be a hero?'

'Dunno.'

She smiled. 'C'mon, Tom. How close was it?'

'For him? I don't know. He'd taken enough pills to knock him out, so I suppose, yes, it was pretty close.'

'Extraordinary coincidence.'

'Extraordinary.'

They didn't need to say much to make themselves understood.

'Of course he'd say it wasn't a coincidence,' Martha went on.

'That's right. Arranged by God.'

'Well, don't knock it,' she said. 'A lot of perfectly rational people would agree with him.'

'Yes, I know. And a lot of perfectly rational people would say it happened that way because Danny planned it.'

'Why would he do that?'

'I don't know. And, anyway, he has to be given the benefit of the doubt. There's no way we're going to prove anything. And outrageous coincidences do happen. He's told you he wants to come and talk to me about . . .' He glanced round, but they had the back room to themselves. The solicitors and barristers who were the Crown's daytime clients preferred the lounge bar. 'The murder.'

'He's been talking about doing that on and off ever

since I've known him. And I've always encouraged him. I think he needs to do it. Whether this is the right time . . .'

'Did you think he was depressed?'

'No. He seemed angry, if anything. But then I suppose if the anger's got nowhere to go . . .'

'How often do you see him?'

'Three times a week.'

Tom whistled. 'That's a helluva lot.'

'Yes, well, he needs it.'

'Do you find him difficult?'

'Draining. Sometimes after I've seen him I have to go home and lie down. But actually he's also quite rewarding. He's . . . I don't know. Very empathic. At times it's almost uncanny. You think, how the hell could he know that? I haven't said anything.' She paused to think. 'He gets inside.'

'Like a tapeworm, you mean?'

'To-om.'

'All right. I was starting to think *I* might consult *him*. So anyway, you think I should do it?'

To his surprise she didn't answer immediately. 'I'm not sure. You know I said he was very good with people? Well, he is, but –'

'He doesn't like triangles.'

She looked surprised. 'How did you know that?'

'Just a hunch.'

'Did he say anything?'

She was over-involved. 'About you? No.'

'Well, anyway, you're quite right, he doesn't. Mike Freeman – you know Mike? – and I were supposed to work together, they thought it would be good for him to have a man and a woman. And it simply wasn't possible.'

'It must've been quite bad if he actually split you?'

'Yeah, well, Mike isn't very experienced.'

He had split them. 'And you think the same thing might happen with you and me?'

'It's possible.'

'I don't really see what you're worried about. So okay, he's not good at triangles? The general idea is that we're supposed to be.'

'It's not just that. There's a certain amount of antagonism there, Tom. Towards you.'

'Yes, I think I detected that. Does he say why?'

'He trusted you. In his mind, you let him down quite badly. He thinks if it wasn't for you, he wouldn't have been in court at all, he'd have been dealt with as a child. You were the one who said he understood what he was doing and that he was fit to plead in an adult court. He hasn't forgiven you.'

Tom nodded. 'We'd need to talk about it. But the antagonism itself isn't automatically a barrier. I mean, frankly, even if I was starting from scratch, I'd expect to be on the receiving end of a fair bit of hostility, because he's angry. He hates the system, he hates what it did to him.'

Martha shook her head. 'No, it's more than that.'

A long pause. Tom said, 'There's no question of my going ahead without your approval.'

'And I think he needs to do it. So that's that, then.'

'You could try getting him to talk to somebody else.'

'I have.' She smiled. 'It's you or nobody.'

'Which raises doubts about his motivation.'

She hesitated. 'He wants to get at the truth, Tom. I've no doubt about that.'

He looked at her. 'You're very concerned about him, aren't you?'

'Over-involved, you mean?'

Tom smiled. 'How much is over? I don't know.'

'I'm concerned about you, as well. What do you want to do next? What do you want me to tell him?'

'I need to see him again. And I'd quite like that to be in your office. You know, establish a fairly formal framework.'

'All right. Normally I don't see him there, because . . . because Ian hasn't got a record, for one thing.'

'I suppose you do know how bad for him that is?'

'But there's no choice, Tom. If the press found him, his life wouldn't be worth living.' She picked up her bag. 'Anyway, I'll fix something up, and give you a ring. Oh and by the way, if you ever phone the office, you will remember he's Ian Wilkinson, won't you?'

He nodded. 'Though he's got to be Danny with me.'

'Yes, I know. Well, I think he'll welcome that.'

★

Talking to Ian on the phone, half an hour later, she was fully aware of how much he welcomed it. 'Dr Seymour hasn't said he's going to do it,' she warned.

'No, I know. But he will.'

She put the phone down, thought about ringing Tom with suggested times, then thought she wouldn't disturb him yet. The cursor on the computer screen winked at her. She felt slightly sick, a combination of VDU glare and sunshine coming through the window. That day she went to fetch Ian back from the prison it had rained as if it would never stop. A smell of wet clothes, condensation on the windows closing them in, a constant patter of drops on the sunroof, and herself, hunched forward over the wheel, trying to see out through windscreen wipers that seemed only to spread the dirt more evenly across the glass. She leant back in her chair, with her hands over her face, and gradually the hum of the computer was replaced by the rhythmic squeak and whine of the wipers moving to and fro.

It had been late evening by the time she reached the prison. Ian was sitting in the waiting room, looking lost. 'You don't half put yourself through it, don't you?' she'd said.

He shook his head without speaking. The street lamps were on as she drove away. Rain bounced on the pavements. In the town she would have said it was dark, but out on the moors you realize what darkness is.

Rain, endless rain, and mist. The snow posts by the side of the road flashed past, inducing an almost trance-like state. She would have welcomed conversation, if only to keep her awake, but Ian remained silent. The mist thickened. They were driving along a narrow road with a steep drop on the left. When she cornered, the headlamps swept across a hillside with heather and clumps of gorse and, scattered here and there, huge grey boulders. Erratic blocks they were called, she remembered, dredging up some geography lesson of long ago.

Ian opened the window to throw his cigarette out, and drops of rain blew into her face. She heard the clank of bells on sheep grazing by the side of the road. In this light they looked like lumps of clotted mist, and any one of them could wander out into the middle of the road. As much as the rain and mist they forced her to slow down.

Ian was angry. That curious blocked anger of his. Knowing he wasn't the victim, knowing he had no right to be angry, and yet seething anyway. She felt his anger in the silence, heard it in the hiss he made drawing on the next cigarette. My God, and she thought *she* smoked too much. It was making her want one, though. 'Could you get me one of mine?' she asked.

She was aware of the rasp and flare of the match. Why not a lighter? she wondered. But no, always matches. She saw his hands, briefly, in the orange glow. Then he put the cigarette into her mouth, his fingers brushing her lips. Watch it, she thought, and hardly knew whether the warning was directed at Ian or herself.

Still silence. It was getting on her nerves, and she needed to concentrate. The road wasn't just wet – it was greasy from the long hot summer. At that last corner she'd felt the car start to skid. Corrected immediately, but it was a nasty shock.

'Do you mind if we stop?' Ian asked abruptly.

'No, I could do with a break.'

She pulled up in the next passing bay and got out. Ian disappeared round a bend in the road, and she walked up and down, smoking and shivering and being rude to the sheep. After a while the darkness, the loneliness, the clunk–clunk of the sheep bells began to get to her, and she looked at the brow of the hill, impatient for Ian's return.

Then the oddity of it struck her. Here she was, a woman alone and nervous on a dark road at night, looking forward to the reappearance of a convicted murderer. She'd never thought of Ian like that – well, yes, perhaps before she met him. But she'd never felt threatened, and in her job she did feel threatened, now and then. Hell, she didn't just *feel* threatened, she *was* threatened – though she'd learnt how to recognize anger seething below the surface, to spot the signs of impending violence, to know when to back off.

Plenty of anger bubbling now, and nowhere to back off to. Extraordinary – she'd just this moment been thinking how she'd never felt threatened by Ian, and yet here she was – not frightened, nowhere near frightened – but certainly tense. She could have done without the sheep and their bloody bells, and the racket they made cropping the grass. Her footsteps, crunching up and down the gravelled passing bay, were beginning to rattle her. Where was he, for God's sake?

She stayed still, and listened. Immediately she heard his footsteps coming towards the brow of the hill. A light seemed to be growing in the distance and, seconds later, she heard the sound of an approaching car. Ian appeared, head and shoulders first, climbing steadily, his shadow, cast by the car's headlights, reaching out towards her, lengthening as he reached the summit. He was nothing, nothing she recognized. A dark figure haloed in light. She waited, and couldn't speak.

'Sorry I've been so long,' he said. 'Just had to get out and walk, you know. I can't sit still when I'm like this.'

And immediately he was Ian. Except that he wasn't Ian. As they waited for the car to pass, she was aware that a line had been crossed in her thinking about him. Until tonight, she would have said without hesitation that he had changed, that he was no longer the same person who had killed Lizzie Parks, or rather she believed that he'd changed. Those few minutes alone on the dark hillside taught her something, not about him, but about herself. He might have changed, but she didn't believe it. Not absolutely. Not without doubt.

And almost as though he'd read her thoughts, Ian started to talk about how impossible it was to leave the past behind. Being turned away from the prison like that was the final straw. He was beginning to think – well, not beginning, he'd thought it for a long time, only he kept pushing it to the back of his mind – that he was going to have to confront the past, in some way, try to make sense of it, before he could move on.

'Perhaps you should see somebody,' Martha said.

'You mean a shrink?'

'Or a psychologist. I don't think it matters as long as you trust them. I mean, in the end, unless you're suffering from an actual mental illness, schizophrenia or something like that, it's the quality of the person that counts. You need to feel safe.'

'I hate shrinks.'

The car splashed into a puddle by the side of the road, and, for a second, the windscreen was marbled, opaque. Christ, she thought. 'Why do you?'

'Dunno. Dad, I suppose. He always used to say you're all right as long as you stay away from them. You can be drunk every night, shit your pants, doesn't matter, but the minute you go to one of them, that's it, you're finished. After that you're just a bag of shite.'

Now that's a helpful instance of father–son bonding, Martha thought. 'Well, perhaps that was your father's experience. But –'

'My own wasn't marvellous.'

'I thought you didn't see anybody?'

'I saw Dr Seymour. That was enough.'

'But that was for an assessment . . .'

'Yes – and his assessment landed me in court. And his evidence landed me in prison. Well done, Dr Seymour.'

They were driving into a valley now. The headlights revealed a huddle of farm buildings, their bricks turned sombre red by the rain.

'And anyway, I don't want treatment. I don't need it. I just want to talk to somebody.'

'I'll ask around.'

She felt, rather than saw, him smile. 'What are you going to ask, Martha? How are you with murderers?'

That word, said flatly, was enough to bring the fear – no, she wouldn't admit to fear – the anxiety thudding back. 'I'll ask around, try to find out who's leak-proof,' she said. 'It should be all of them, but it isn't.'

'No, well, wives get told. Secretaries. Girlfriends.' He was smiling again. 'Better not do it at all.'

'No, I think it's a good idea.'

They were behind a long vehicle that was sending up arcs of spray and grit on either side, and trailing a white rag from a girder sticking out at the rear. Martha pulled out to overtake. The spray hit the windscreen, and for a few seconds she drove blind, until they pulled clear and the lorry dwindled in the rear-view mirror.

'Decisive driving,' Ian said. He hadn't moved.

The rush of adrenalin loosened Martha's tongue. 'It's not fair, blaming Dr Seymour for your conviction.'

'Who else should I blame?'

'How about the police who collected the evidence? The pathologist who examined it, the judge who summed up, or the jury who brought in the verdict?'

'No, no, no, no, no, no. Dr Seymour. I'd have been acquitted if it hadn't been for him.'

No point arguing. It was insane.

'You think I'm mad, don't you?' Almost crooning the words, he went on, 'But they believed me, Martha. They did. I know they did.' His tone hardened. 'I trusted him.'

Martha wanted to ask, Are you saying you didn't do it? She kept quiet, distrusting her motives for doing so. If they'd been somewhere else, somewhere less isolated, would she have challenged him?

Ian brooded. 'It was a disgraceful performance.'

It was bad for him to slip into thinking of himself as the victim, and yet she'd never met anybody who thought the Lizzie Parks murder trial had been handled well. It was difficult for him not to feel victimized.

'These aren't your memories, are they, Ian?'

He glanced sideways. 'Ian hasn't got any memories.'

'It doesn't help to say things like that.'

'No, they're not memories. I got the transcripts through my solicitor.'

Now, hot and nauseous in the sunlit office, Martha sifted through her memories of that night. Events had moved on. He had something to thank Tom for now, after the coincidence of Tom's being the one to rescue him from the river.

Martha twisted from side to side. Her chair might as well have had spikes in the seat. Coincidences do happen, she told herself. People travel to the other side of the world, and find themselves standing in a queue next to somebody who lives in the same street. It happens all the time. Well, obviously, not *all* the time, or nobody would exclaim over it, but it does happen. No point saying you don't believe in coincidence. But she'd have found it easier to believe in this one if she hadn't heard the hatred in Ian's voice in the car.

Hatred? No, wrong word. Something more painful than that. Betrayed trust. A sense of something good gone disastrously wrong. Whatever it was, she'd been left in no doubt that Tom was the last person Ian would go to for help. And yet, less than a month later, he'd become the only person. And she didn't know why.

EIGHT

Tom arrived at the probation office ten minutes early, to find that Martha had had to dash out to see another client. He spent the time till Danny arrived pacing up and down the small waiting room. It turned out that Martha shared her office, and both interview rooms were occupied, so he was going to have to see Danny here.

The room reeked of sweat: the accumulated total of the perspiring and anxious humanity that had squeezed into it. Polystyrene cups with grey coffee dregs, and holes burnt in the sides where illicit cigarettes had been stubbed out. A 'No Smoking' sign hung on the wall above the blocked-up fireplace, but the regular visitors to this room were not known for abiding by the rules.

He heard footsteps in the corridor. A young woman's voice – the receptionist's – and then a murmur, without distinguishable words: Danny. He came into the room quickly, smiling and holding out his hand.

Tom waited until he was settled in his chair. 'Well, I've spoken to Martha, and we thought it would be a good idea if you and I met and had another chat, and then you could decide if you wanted to go ahead, or not.'

'I've decided. I thought this was to help you.'

Tom let that pass. 'I've been thinking back to when I was ten, trying to work out what I remember. And the thing that strikes me is that I probably don't remember . . . You know, the important things, the kind of things my parents would remember. The memories are quite vivid, I was surprised at how much I remembered, but they're . . . memories of a child's world. And I've been wondering how much you remember.'

Danny cleared his throat. 'Quite a bit.'

'For instance, the time I came to see you in the remand centre. What do you remember about that?'

'You wanted me to play with dolls. I thought, Christ, if this gets out, I'm dead.'

'Nothing else?'

'I remember you. And of course one or two things I said were quoted in court.'

A slight edge to his voice. 'Did that surprise you?'

'Yes. Because I thought it was confidential.'

'But an assessment can't be confidential. It's designed to be produced in court.'

'I know. But I was ten, and nobody told me that.'

'So you felt –'

Danny was groping for his cigarettes, but then he saw the notice over the fireplace and put the packet back.

'What did you feel, Danny? Betrayed?'

A deep breath, caught and held. 'Yes.'

'I'm sorry.'

Danny spread his hands.

'Did you know why I was there?'

'I knew you were meant to find out whether I was . . . mental? I don't know. Round the twist? Bonkers? Crazy? I don't know what word I'd have used. But, yeah, I knew why you were there, only of course in my mind it was a pretty pointless exercise because I hadn't done it anyway.'

'Are you saying you didn't do it?'

'No, I'm saying I believed I hadn't. I believed my own story. I had to.'

'And at the trial?'

'I still believed it. I went to the house to see a litter of kittens, I found Lizzie dead on the floor, and there was a man walking about upstairs. I ran like hell, and didn't tell anybody because I was too frightened. That was it. That was what happened.'

'What else do you remember? About the trial.'

'Just being bored. I was so bored my mind ached. I used to look at the clock, and the minute-hand jerked, you know, it didn't move smoothly, and I used to wait for the next jerk. I wasn't allowed to play with anything, because, I think, if they'd given me toys to play with, they'd have been admitting a whole lot of things. I was always being told to sit up straight, listen, look at the person who's speaking, and half the time I didn't understand a word.'

'So what do you remember?'

He took a moment to think. 'The judge, because of his robes and his wig. Do you know, I still . . . if there's something in a room that's bright red, I sit with my back to it, or put it somewhere I can't see it? And that comes from the trial.'

'Anything else?'

'Playing squiggles with one of the warders. This was in the lunch hour. You know, one person draws a squiggle, and the other has to try to turn it into something. I took the paper into court with me, and the social worker scrumpled it up and threw it away. What else? I remember my father sneaking out for a fag, because his shoes squeaked, and he sort of tiptoed out, and the more he tiptoed the more they squeaked. I used to hate that.'

'Anything else?'

'I remember you. I used to look at you. And I remember you saying all that about the chicken. If you wring a chicken's neck, you don't expect to see it running round the yard next day, do you? And everybody went . . .' A sudden, audible intake of breath. 'That was the moment. They didn't believe I'd done it till then.'

'And you really think they convicted you on that?'

'Yes.'

Tom smiled, patiently. 'I don't think it was as simple as that, Danny. There was a lot of forensic evidence.'

'Yes, but they didn't believe it. They believed me.'

The defence had put Danny into the witness box. God knows how they'd summoned up the courage to do it, but they had. He was superb. He began well, by being good-looking, but he also stood up straight, spoke clearly, didn't fidget, made eye contact, appeared confident (but never cocky), and remembered to address the judge as 'My Lord' and counsel as 'Sir'. He gave the impression he was telling the truth, and indeed he was − 98 per cent of the time. Altogether, he came over as the sort of boy you'd be proud to introduce as your nephew.

Tom had looked at him across the courtroom, and thought, How can so many things be right?

The jury had been impressed. But to say that they'd believed his story was ridiculous. Of course they hadn't. There'd been too much hard evidence to contradict it. 'No, you're not remembering it accurately, Danny. It wasn't like that.'

Danny shrugged. 'It was, you know. But don't let's argue about it. I'm not blaming you. You did the best you could in the circumstances.'

Tom remembered the courtroom, the stillness as he stepped into the box. 'I think by that time I just wanted it to be over. I wanted to get you out of there and into treatment.'

'Yeah, well, that didn't happen.'

'I wrote to the Home Office, but I got the standard brush-off.'

A pause. Tom was massaging the skin of his forehead, as he always did when he was stressed. 'You know the English teacher you mentioned? Tell me a little bit more about him.'

'Angus MacDonald,' Danny said, in a broad Scottish accent. 'He was . . . a very, very good teacher, and I started writing little bits and pieces for him. Extra stuff, not just in the classroom. About animals on the farm, that sort of thing. Then it got on to my parents, and . . .' He took a deep breath. 'Various things that happened.'

'But not the murder?'

'No.' Danny paused to wipe sweat off his upper lip. 'Look, after the trial I spent one night in prison, proper grown-up prison, there was nowhere else for me to go, and it absolutely stank – piss and cabbage. And I thought – nobody told me anything – I thought, This is it. And then next day the Greenes turned up and took me to Long Garth. And after I was settled in, Mr Greene came and sat on the bed, and he said – I can't remember the exact words obviously, but it was all to do with putting the past behind me. Just forget it. And that was that, and because I admired him – and because I was shocked out of my skull – I tried to do it. I lived for four years in this sort of eggshell, until Angus came along and smashed it. And he was *right*. Even then, I knew he was right, but, at the same time, I was scared out of my wits by it.'

'So what happened?'

'Nothing happened. He left. It was only a temporary appointment anyway.'

There was a story here, Tom thought, and he wasn't being told it. 'And he left before you got to the murder?'

'Yes.'

'And no more attempts after that?'

'In prison I joined a therapy group. Which was pathetic. Load of wankers telling the same lies they'd told in court. But the guy in charge had one really good idea, or anyway I thought so. He used to give people a tape recorder and tell them to say whatever they wanted, let it all . . . you know, spew out, and the only rule was you had to burn the tape at the end. I really liked the idea of that. So I got the tape recorder, and off I went, and . . . you were sort of supervised. There was somebody outside the room. And I couldn't say a bloody word. I just sat there and watched it going round.'

'What was going through your mind?'

'Frustration. And then I started to think perhaps it wasn't such a good idea. I mean, what's to stop somebody bullshitting from beginning to end? You know . . .' His voice became an aggressive whine. ' "It wasn't really my fault, other people had a lot to do with it, I've had a hard life . . ." Why would somebody tell the truth just because they're talking to themselves? That's the world's most uncritical audience. You need somebody who can say, "Hey, c'mon, it wasn't like that." A sort of a . . .'

'Bullshit detector?'

'Yeah, something like that. A reality checker.'

'And you couldn't do that with the therapist?'

'No, he only did group work. And anyway . . .'

Danny stopped, and for a moment Tom thought he wasn't going to go on. But then, looking out of the window, he said, 'Whenever I've imagined myself trying to talk about it, it's always been with you.'

'Because I was there?'

'Yes, I suppose so.'

'I can see it might make things easier.'

'No, not easier. But the thing is, I can be Danny with you. I can't be Danny with anybody else.'

Tom said slowly, 'I'm surprised you still trust me.'

'You mean, because the last time I spilled the beans it all came out in court?'

'If you think you "spilled the beans", Danny . . . You were the most self-contained, wary kid I'd ever met.'

'There, you see? That's exactly what I need. Somebody who knows what it was like.'

'I wasn't there most of the time.'

'No, but you'd know if I was lying. To myself, I mean. Obviously, I won't be lying to you.' He laughed. 'No point.' Despite the laughter, he was

99

sweating. Suddenly, he stood up. 'Do you mind if I pop out for a bit? I need a cigarette.'

Tom held out a polystyrene cup with cigarette butts floating on the dregs.

'Yeah, I know, but . . .' He jerked his head at the 'No Smoking' sign. 'I'm a good boy, I am.'

That smile, Tom thought, as the door closed behind him. It was enough to make an atheist believe in damnation.

Restless, he got up and went across to the window, wishing that he too could escape from the fetid little room, but reluctant to leave, in case Danny came back and found him gone. There wasn't too much antagonism there, he thought. Some. Probably rather more than Danny admitted, but not enough to matter. The fact was, anybody trying to help Danny would need a pretty robust identity to cope with some of the things he was likely to throw at them. He wasn't looking forward to it, but he'd decided to do it. In the end, the question was not whether he would take Danny on, but whether he was prepared to abandon him. This wasn't the start of a professional relationship, but the continuation of one that had begun thirteen years ago.

The smell in this room was intolerable. Tom went to the door and flung it open, only to see Danny coming along the narrow corridor towards him, head down, striding along as if he were in open country.

Baulked of his need to escape, Tom retreated into the room, and sat down. 'Better?'

'Yeah,' Danny said, with an apologetic smile. 'Filthy habit, can't kick it.'

'Is that the only one?'

Danny blinked. 'Apart from temazepam, yes.'

'I just want to get one or two things straight. Have you seen a transcript of the trial?'

'Yes.'

'Do you think that's confused your own memories?'

'No, it didn't have any impact at all. It was too different. Anyway, it's the . . . It's not the trial I want to talk about.'

'So we'll be focusing on your childhood. Well, the bit of your childhood that came before . . .'

'That's all of it. There wasn't much childhood after.'

'What we talk about is entirely up to you. I might ask you to fill in something I'm not clear about, but that's all. Basically, you decide. Is that all right?'

'Fine.'

'The other thing is, do you mind if I talk to other people? Obviously, I won't repeat anything you tell me.' He saw Danny smile. 'No, this time the confidentiality *is* absolute. Only, if I were going to talk to other people, I'd probably need to tell them you were seeing me. Is that all right?'

Danny was shaking his head.

'It's entirely up to you.'

'I don't want my father involved. As far as I know he doesn't know where I am, and that suits me fine.'

'I was thinking of the headmaster at Long Garth.'

'Mr Greene?' He looked surprised. 'Yeah, all right. I don't mind that.'

'All right, then. One more thing. *If* I think you're becoming more depressed as a result of the sessions, we're going to have to think very carefully about whether we go on.'

'I don't want to start, and then give up.'

'No, but there're all kinds of compromises. I was thinking twice a week initially, but if things get a bit tough there's no reason why you can't take a week out. All I'm saying is we need to be flexible.'

'All right. I do want to get on with it, though.'

'I'll have a word with Martha, and as soon as I've done that we can arrange a time.'

'Okay.'

Danny seemed subdued now, bracing himself perhaps. The moment Tom made a move, he stood up and held out his hand. As Tom took it, he was remembering the embrace that had ended their first meeting, the child's hot, sticky face pressed into his midriff. And then the warder's comment: 'Well, he is a horror, isn't he?' echoing in his head, as he walked back to his car, where, waiting for him, spilling out of the file and over the back seat, were the photographs of Lizzie Parks, the horror of the images impossible to connect with the child he'd just left.

Danny was right, in one way. He did need to do this. He needed to make the connection.

NINE

It was nonsense what Danny had said about the trial, and Tom knew it was nonsense. He had an adult memory of the proceedings and Danny did not. Simple as that. But Danny's words niggled away at him, nevertheless. Along with other problems. Lauren was proving difficult to contact, and that had to be deliberate. Often when he phoned, she was out, and she didn't reply to messages left on the answering machine. When he did succeed in getting through to her, she was remote and monosyllabic. The book too had reached a sticky patch, when he simply had to stop and do some more research before he could move on again. Nothing much was going right, but he just had to put his head down and get on with it.

He spent the morning after his interview with Danny in the medical library, looking up papers on the microfiche. He hated the machines, which produced, if he persisted in using them long enough, visual disturbances that resembled a migraine, though without pain. By the time he left the library, feeling physically and mentally sick, he knew he was in for one of them. The sunlight flashing on windscreens and bumpers hurt his eyes. By the time he got to his car, there was a dark spot at the centre of his field of vision in his right eye, surrounded by a halo of tarnished silver light. He moved his head, as he always did, trying to get rid of it, though he knew it was pointless. The black circle moved with his head. A patch of temporary ischaemia on the surface of his retina. As a boy he'd been fascinated by it, because he was looking at the absence of sight, and the paradox pleased him. Now it was merely a nuisance.

Since it wasn't safe to drive he had to sit in the hot car till it was over. It lasted about ten minutes. After the last flashing light had faded, he sat with his head in his hands, feeling totally washed up. For some reason, despite the absence of pain and vomiting, and all the more distressing aspects of a migraine, these episodes exhausted him. Yet he felt the world was a new place. He looked round the car park, and his unimpeded vision made every object he saw miraculous.

On the spur of the moment he decided to phone Nigel Lewis, who had been Danny's solicitor at the time of the trial. Phone pressed to his ear, he leant against the side of the car, fully expecting to be told that Mr Lewis was in court and unavailable for the rest of the day. Instead he came on the line at once.

After exchanging greetings, Tom said, 'You remember Daniel Miller?'

'Miller? I don't think —'

Tom could hear a conversation going on in the
background. 'Yes, you do,' he insisted, trying not
to sound impatient, as Nigel put a hand over the
mouthpiece and made some apologetic remark to the
other people in the room. 'The murder of Lizzie
Parks. He was ten, remember?'

'*Miller?* Oh God, yes. Of course I remember.'

'Well, he's out. He came to see me the other day.'

Another aside to the people in the room.

'Look, can we talk?' Tom asked. 'I mean, can we
meet somewhere?'

'Cooperage? One o'clock?'

'Fine.' It was almost that now.

The Quayside never failed to lift Tom's spirits, no
matter how low his mood when he arrived. He leant
on the railings for a few minutes, listening to gulls cry
and grizzle, watching the tough, brown, sinewy river
flow under the bridge and on towards the sea. You
could smell the sea on windy days like this, imagine
cliffs crumbling, the coast nibbled away, big concrete
tank traps, eroded by spring and neap tides, blown as
specks of grit into the eye.

Nigel, a great believer in liquid lunches, had arrived
first and was already standing at the bar, holding his
usual pint of lager. 'I nearly ordered for you,' he said,
as Tom went up to him.

'Thanks, I will have one.'

'So. What's the matter?' Nigel said, as they set their pints down on a table at the far end of the bar.

'Nothing's the matter, he —'

'So did he just show up? How long's he been out?'

'Nearly a year.'

Nigel lifted the glass to his mouth. 'Oh well, I suppose they couldn't keep him in for ever.'

'You're not his solicitor any more?'

'No, thank God. So anyway what happened?'

'We bumped into each other. And then he decided it might be helpful if he talked to somebody.'

'Helpful to him, of course. Figures.'

'I've said I'll see him.'

'Why?'

'Curiosity, I suppose. Partly. It's not often you get the chance to follow up a case like that.' He smiled. 'It's not often you get a case like that.'

'But he's not a patient? I mean, you're —'

'Oh no, no. He's made it perfectly plain he doesn't want treatment. He just wants to talk.'

Nigel smiled his well-oiled smile. 'I suppose it'd be quite a feather in your cap to write that one up, wouldn't it?'

No point trying to explain to Nigel the effect of Danny's hot face against his stomach all those years ago. Nigel focused on the lowest common denominator of human behaviour, and over the years had become totally, devastatingly cynical. Which left him, Tom thought, not merely blind to the more-than-occasional goodness of human beings, but to the evil as well. His was a world where people looked after number one, and kept an eye on the main chance. He seemed unable to grasp that some people act out of a disinterested love of destruction. Evil, be thou my good . . . That had been left out of his repertoire. He was lucky.

'No, I don't think I'll be doing that. It was something he said, it's been bothering me a bit. I mean – briefly, he said it was my evidence that convicted him – and of course I reminded him about the forensic evidence, and all that, but . . . he didn't bat an eyelid. He simply said, "No. It was you."'

'Hmm. Sounds as if he's read a transcript.'

This was not the response Tom had expected. Nigel put down his lager, wiped his mouth discreetly on the back of his hand and sat back on the bench seat, looking grave. Tom ought, perhaps, to have welcomed this evidence that he was being taken seriously, that his anxiety had not automatically been dismissed as groundless, but he didn't. He wanted his concern taken seriously, and the grounds for it dismissed. Nigel's response was just exasperating.

'You sure you bumped into him?' Nigel asked. 'He didn't come looking for you?'

Tom was not going to mention the attempted suicide, the coincidence of their meeting again like that. He knew, anyway, what Nigel would have said. Instead, he reverted to Danny's remark about Tom's evidence having convicted him, recalling details of the case, reminding Nigel of the vast quantity of forensic evidence that had linked Danny to the crime, the fact that he'd been missing from school that day, the eye-witnesses who'd seen him running away from Lizzie Parks's house. He was beginning to gabble, to make sarcastic remarks, anything to get Nigel to say of course it was ridiculous. He desperately needed Nigel to say that his evidence had merely confirmed what the jury knew already, but Nigel remained ominously silent. 'You know, I almost get the feeling he thinks he wouldn't have been convicted if it hadn't been for me.'

'Oh, that's putting it a bit strong.'

'A bit strong?'

'I don't like the sound of this, Tom. You don't have to see him, surely?'

'No, it's –'

'And if he starts pestering you, all you have to do is to tell the Home Office. He'll be back inside in no time. That's one thing you can say about the system. They're on a very short leash.' He raised his glass to his lips, pausing to add: 'Thank God.'

'I suppose what I want from you is some sort of reassurance that it's not true. I mean, I've always assumed my contribution was . . . trivial, really, and what actually convicted him was the forensic evidence.'

Nigel didn't actually squirm on the bench, because he was too bulky for his movements to be interpreted in that way. 'Ye-es, but you know the forensic evidence really only connected him to the scene, and he didn't deny being there. He didn't deny touching her, he didn't deny lifting the cushion off her face. There was nothing really conclusive. It's not as if she had claw marks all over her face and he had her skin under his fingernails.'

'But his fingerprints were all over the bedroom.'

'The kittens were in the bedroom. He'd been to see the kittens twice – or so he said. Lizzie wasn't around to deny it. The point is, Tom, the jury believed him. You know how long I hesitated about putting him in the box. I wasn't frightened he was going to crack under the pressure and tell a pack of stupid lies – I knew he wouldn't. I thought he'd come across as an arrogant little bastard – which he was. But in the event it paid off. He stood up straight, he looked them in the eye, he was well turned out, admitted that, yes, he'd been a naughty boy, he'd nicked off school, yes, he'd gone to the house, but only to see the kittens, and he was utterly devastated when he found the body. And when he saw the naughty man at the top of the stairs, he was frightened, he thought the naughty man was going to kill him, and so he didn't tell anybody. Mad piece of behaviour in an adult, totally normal in a ten-year-old. I was looking at them all the way through. They believed him, Tom. They looked at that kid, and they didn't believe he'd done it. I didn't believe it, and I knew he had.'

'And I convinced them he had?'

'You convinced them he was capable of it. By the time Smithers was through with you, you'd told them that Danny was capable of distinguishing between fantasy and reality . . .' Nigel was counting points off on his fingers. 'Fully understood that killing somebody was seriously wrong, not just naughty. Fully understood that death was a permanent, irreversible state. Now I'm not saying you were wrong, but none of that helped Danny. By the time you'd finished what they had in their minds was not a nice little boy, but a precocious little killer.'

'You didn't say anything at the time.'

'What was the point? You did the best you could for the kid, under very nasty hostile cross-examination. Smithers went right over the top that day. A lot of people more experienced than you would've been wilting by the end. I thought it was disgraceful. You're not supposed to treat an expert witness as hostile, and he came very, very close. I remember Duncan sitting back in his chair at one point, and saying, "Well, that's it, then. We can all go home." And he threw his pencil down on the pad.'

Duncan had been the defence counsel. 'As bad as that?'

'I don't know about bad. The fact is the little bugger ended up inside. Which was the right outcome.'

'I didn't see it like that. I didn't think my evidence had any particular impact.'

'Oh, it did. But there's always a moment in a long trial when the thing swings. Juries aren't rational, the seats are too hard, the room's too hot, it goes on for days and days and bloody days. Weeks. Do you know the average person's attention span is *twenty minutes*? And they'd listened to Danny for hours. I think they rather admired him in a funny sort of way. I know I did. But you could see them thinking, I don't know, he seems all right . . . And then you came along, and you supplied them with another perspective.'

'I didn't change a single fact.'

'No, but you changed the way they saw him. You scuppered him. And I can tell you the exact moment it happened. Smithers was asking you whether Danny understood that death was a permanent state. Do you remember? And you quoted Danny's exact words. "If you wring a chicken's neck, you don't expect to see it running round the yard next morning."'

'But he was talking about chickens. He lived on a chicken farm, for Christ's sake!'

'Doesn't matter. And everybody went . . .' He mimicked the intake of breath, exactly as Danny had done.

'Danny remembers that.'

'Does he?' Nigel said. 'That's interesting.'

Tom was thinking. 'I suppose I've never been easy about it, because Smithers got me on the ropes. I know he did. There was no hope of qualifying anything – he just swept it aside.'

Nigel grunted. 'I wouldn't blame yourself too much. All you did was quote his own words.'

'He wasn't referring to Lizzie.'

'It was the attitude. All that about it didn't really matter because she was old, she'd had her life. You ripped the mask off, and okay, you lost me the case.' He shrugged. 'I'm glad somebody did, because if he hadn't been caught he'd have done it again.'

'Do you really believe that?'

'Of course. He was on to a good thing, wasn't he? Befriending old ladies, robbing them, and if they got in the way – splat! I think you should pat yourself on the back. And if you have any bother at all with him, tell the police.'

Tom sat lost in thought, until a discreet movement from Nigel drew his attention to their empty glasses. He roused himself to go to the bar, where he ordered another pint for Nigel and a half for himself.

He got back to the table to find Nigel chatting to two barristers, and the conversation necessarily changed to other topics.

Half an hour later, as they were leaving the pub, Nigel fell deliberately behind and drew Tom aside. 'Look, don't let him get to you. You told the truth. And as far as I'm concerned the only mistake's the Home Office letting the little bugger out.'

He nodded, and hurried to catch up with his colleagues, a shoal of dark fish weaving in amongst the brightly dressed crowd.

TEN

Danny replaced the burnt matchstick carefully in the box.

Tom said, 'I've been thinking about that English teacher of yours. What was his name again?'

Danny looked wary. 'Angus MacDonald.'

'You were close?'

'Yes, I suppose. Ish.' He tapped ash off his cigarette. 'It was a long time ago.'

Silence, except for the pop-pop of the gas fire, and the wind slamming against the windows.

'You know,' Danny said suddenly, 'all day I've been thinking I can't go through with this, and now I think I can.' He glanced at the red-shaded lamp on Tom's desk. 'I don't know where to start.'

'You said with Angus you started with little things. About the farm.'

'Yes . . .'

'Worked, then.'

'Yeah, all right. The first thing I ever wrote for him

started with me in bed on a winter's night watching reflections on the wall, hearing people outside in the yard, shouting, calling. Feeling, you know, exiled – the way kids do when they're in bed and everything's still going on downstairs.'

'Whose voices are they?'

'My mother's. Fiona's – that's the girl who used to work for us. Sometimes my father's – not often. He was generally in the pub by then.'

'And what are they doing?'

'Putting the hens away for the night. We had some free-range hens. It wasn't *free*, exactly, but it was better than the batteries. I used to go into the batteries with my mother, and there were all these heads poking out, bright eyes, these jerky little movements, coxcombs jiggling. I'd be walking along the aisle like this.' He hunched his arms together across his chest. 'I was afraid of being pecked. I don't know why, because I'd been pecked dozens of times. They didn't live long. When they got past the point of no return, Dad used to wring their necks. Sometimes he'd swing them so they hit me in the face.'

'Why do you think he did that?'

'Oh, I'd be pulling faces. I didn't like it. We used to have pullets in runs in one of the fields, and there was this little skinny white pullet and the others started pecking it. All the feathers had come out, its skin was red raw, and Dad said he'd have to kill it. I didn't want him to. I said, "Can't we put it in another run by itself until it gets bigger?"' A deep breath. 'So he made me do it.'

'How?'

'How did he make me? I don't know. I knew I had to. You know, you just pull and twist and . . .' Small, foetal movements of the hands. 'The eyes cloud over.'

'How old were you?'

'Six.' He caught Tom's expression. 'Yeah, well, he was on this great toughen-up-the-lad campaign. Perhaps he was right, perhaps I needed it.'

'What makes you think that?'

'Until I was five, there was Mum and me and her parents. Dad was in the army.'

'Why didn't you live on the base?'

'We did, to begin with. I was born in Germany, but Mum got depressed after the birth. Apparently he used to come home, and I'd be screaming in one room and she'd be slumped in a chair. More or less in the same position she'd been in when he left. I think she just about fed me and kept me clean, but that was it. And then he had to go to Northern Ireland, and of course the families can't go with them there. So she came home to her parents. I think it was meant to be temporary, but once she got away from the base there was no way she was going back.'

'So you didn't see very much of him?'

'He used to come home on leave. I was always glad when he went back. Then he was in the Falklands, then Northern Ireland again, and then suddenly he was home.'

'For good?'

Danny laughed. 'Or evil. Permanently, anyway.'

'What was that like?'

'A cataclysm. For me. I've got two photographs of me round about four, five. One's of me sitting on Mum's knee in a Paddington Bear t-shirt. And the other – this is only two months later – I'm wearing a flak jacket and carrying a gun.'

'Toy gun?'

'No, his. He let me hold it.'

'And you liked that?'

'Yeah, I thought it was great.'

'So there was a change of allegiance?'

'Hmm. Yes, that's exactly the right word.'

Tom thought for a moment. 'What were some of the changes?'

'Well – I'm trying to be fair here – there was a lot of rough and tumble, a lot of charging about and shouting, and . . . I'd never had that, you see. Because although we lived with my grandparents at the time, Granddad was . . . he was almost more of an old woman than Gran.'

'And you liked the games?'

'Most of the time, yes. But he had a very short fuse. We were playing French cricket once and I got hit on the leg and started bawling and he threw the bat at me. And, you know . . . *at* me. I was taken to casualty.

And . . . I don't know why things got worse, but they did.' He was massaging his forehead as he spoke. 'I wasn't the kid he wanted, I think I have to accept that, but I think there was an element of . . . I don't think he was in a terrific state when he got back from the Falklands, and within a month, literally within a month, he was in Northern Ireland.'

'And drinking heavily.'

'Yes. How did you know that?'

'Something you said before. Go on. You said things got worse. How?'

'I started getting the shit beat out of me. He had this big thick black belt. He used to keep it on the table by the television, and . . . If you hadn't done anything too bad, you got the leather end.'

'But not always.'

'No, not always.'

A long silence. Somewhere outside, in a different world, footsteps hurried past.

'I've thought about this a lot. I honestly do believe he thought he was doing the right thing. But he had a temper, and you've got to remember in his mind he was very hard done by. Loved the army, stupid bitch can't cope, sends her home, still can't cope. He comes out of the army – and she still can't cope.'

'So your mother was still depressed?'

'Not while we were living with her parents, I don't think. Later, on the farm, she was. But that would've depressed anybody.'

'And he blamed your mother?'

'For him having to leave the army? Yes.'

'Who did she blame?'

'Herself. I think. That was . . . That was the myth, I suppose. He was doing well in the army, he had to come out because of her, and that was the end of a brilliant career. She believed it, I'm sure she did – I don't think she ever doubted it was all her fault.'

'Was it true?'

A flicker of impatience. 'God knows. I think when it comes to your parents you might as well stick with the myths, because you're never going to get at the truth. It's just not possible. And anyway, it's the myths that form you.'

'I'd still like to hear what you think now.'

A deep sigh. 'Well, before he went into the army he couldn't settle to anything.'

'Sorry. Can I stop you there? Who's this coming from?'

'My grandmother. Who didn't like him, so the source is prejudiced.'

'Your mother?'

'Never said a word against him – ever.'

'Okay, go on.'

'What I think – and this is only suspicion, I don't know – I think he came back from the Falklands in a far worse state than he let on. And perhaps it wasn't altogether unwelcome to have an honourable way of getting out of it. Or perhaps I'm just making excuses and he was a violent bastard who'd have beaten the shit out of me anyway.'

'Did he ever talk about the army?'

'Oh, all the time.'

'With regret?'

'I don't think so. I think the first year on the farm he was quite happy. There was a lot of building, draining fields, that kind of thing, and he liked all that. There was a cowshed, and he turned it into a workshop. Mum never went in there, so it was a sort of den.'

'Did you go?'

'Yes. They were some of the best times. There was one window, so grimed up hardly any light got through, and I'd sit on a bale of straw – it was scratchy on the backs of my legs, still remember it – and watch him hammering away, smoking, always smoking. And his hair was curly, and there'd be a sort of fuzz of sunlight and cigarette smoke round him, and he'd talk about the army. This guy he killed in Belfast. They were clearing houses, and he shot him, and he sort of slid down the wall, very slowly, leaving this broad band of red all the way down the wallpaper. And there was another story from the Falklands – chasing somebody, and when the guy turned round it was a child. Early teens, I suppose, but he didn't look it. He looked about twelve.'

Tom was startled. Danny had slipped into being his father. 'What happened?'

'Killed him. Nothing else to do.'

'Do you remember how he said that?'

'No. I know what you mean. I don't remember. I've asked myself that many a time. You know, was he traumatized? Was he talking to me like he'd have talked to a –' He stopped and shook his head.

'A tape recorder?'

'Dog, I was going to say. But we had a dog, so perhaps you're right.'

'What do you think?'

'I think it's too easy for sensitive types' – Danny's voice oozed contempt – 'to assume that everybody who kills is traumatized by it. I think there's a lot of evidence that the majority of people get used to it quite quickly. And . . . yes, I do think it bothered him that he'd killed a child. But not very much. The kid was in uniform, he had a gun, and the responsibility for his death belongs with the people who put him there. I'm pretty certain that's the way Dad saw it.'

'And what do you think about that?'

'I think he was right.'

'So why did he tell you these stories?'

'Reliving good times? He always . . . you know, although a lot of things happened in the Falklands that disturbed him, he never stopped seeing it as an enormous stroke of luck. In the army, you're mainly rehearsing for something you never do. And he did it. He was grateful for that.'

A pause. Tom said, 'Why did you get beaten? I mean, what sort of things did you do?'

'Breathe.'

'As bad as that?'

'Yes. In the end I couldn't do anything right. I mean, he used to take me rabbiting. I did like it, I liked the occasion, going off with him and Duke. But I didn't like the dead rabbits. "But you'll eat it, won't you?" he used to say, and then he'd shove it in my face. I remember walking back with him once, trailing along behind. Cold, frosty day and these rabbits dangling from his bag. Glazed eyes, blood in their mouths. Feet swinging.'

'What are you feeling?'

'Feeble. No use.' A pause. 'I'm afraid I've lost the thread a bit. I can't remember why I was telling you that. Oh, I know, I couldn't eat the stew, so I got belted for that.'

'What were the best times?'

'Watching videos. He'd have his fags and his cans of beer, and I'd creep closer to him on the sofa. I was always watching him out of the corner of my eye and whatever expression was on his face, I'd try to imitate it.'

'What sort of things did you watch?'

'War movies.' He laughed. 'Of course.'

'Which one do you remember best?'

'*Apocalypse Now*. Saw that three or four times.'

'Isn't that an anti-war movie?'

'Didn't bother him. He just screened out the anti. And he liked some horror films. Good ones. We watched *An American Werewolf* and I was so frightened I hid behind the sofa, and afterwards, days afterwards, I was writing these little notes. You know, block capitals, NOT A REAL WOLF.'

'What do you remember about it? The film.'

'The transformation scene. And . . . oh, it's ages since I've seen it. Umm . . . There's a scene where he's in a cinema, and all along the row there're decomposing corpses. People he's killed, or perhaps other werewolves, I don't know.' He paused. 'I used to have the poster of *Apocalypse Now* in my room at Long Garth. The huge red sun and the choppers. In fact, I'm not sure he didn't buy it for me.'

'Any other good times?'

'Being in the shed watching him make things. Mainly fences, that sort of thing. He used to go out in all weathers. My mother used to say, "You're never going out in that, are you?" And he'd be standing in the kitchen door, and he'd say, "When the going gets tough, the tough get going."' Danny laughed. 'When the going got tough, the tough pissed off.'

Tom let a silence open up, before slipping in, casually, 'Were you an abused child?'

Danny looked startled. 'No. Well, the beatings, I suppose . . .'

'Were they frequent?'

'Yes.'

'Severe?'

'Depends what you mean by severe.'

'Did they leave marks?'

'Yes.'

'Bruises?'

'Yes.'

'Weals?'

'Sometimes.'

'So. Were you abused?'

'I don't know. Do you think I was?'

Tom smiled. 'It doesn't work like that, Danny.'

'Was I abused?' He was massaging his forehead again, this time with his hand hiding most of his face. 'Oh God. I suppose by modern standards, in comparison with most kids, yes. Slightly.'

'That's an incredibly qualified answer.'

'Yes, well, I think it has to be. If it'd been the 1880s – you know, be a man, my son, send forth the best ye breed, and all that – everybody would've thought he was doing a splendid job.'

'But it wasn't.'

'I know, that's what I've just said. By modern standards, probably, yes.'

Tom waited.

'Slightly.'

'Slightly?'

'Yes, *slightly*. I wasn't neglected, sexually abused, starved, tortured, left on my own morning, noon and night, scalded, burnt . . . All of which happens.'

'I know.'

'He was misguided, but he did honestly think he was doing the right thing.'

'What was the worst thing?'

'The worst beating?'

'No, the worst thing. The worst time.'

'Being hung up on a peg. Hung up. Not hanged.'

'Why did he do that?'

'I don't know. I was being obstreperous, I suppose. He lifted me on to the peg, put my jacket over the pegs and left me there to scream.'

'How long for?'

'Not long.' He took a deep breath. 'I'm determined I'm not going to say, "I was abused, therefore . . ." Because it's not as easy as that.'

'No.'

'The fact is he was trying to be a good father, and . . . I hero-worshipped him. He was tall, he was strong, he had a tattoo that wiggled when he clenched his fist, he had a gun, he'd killed people . . . I thought he was fucking brilliant.'

It took Tom a long time to realize that Danny was not using his father's violence as a way of excusing his own behaviour. It was rather more sophisticated than that. He was talking about moral circles, the group of people (and animals) inside the circle, whom it is not permissible to kill, and the others, outside, who enjoy no such immunity. For Danny's father, dogs, cats and most people were inside the circle. Chickens, convicted murderers, rabbits, enemy soldiers, farm animals, enemy civilians (in some circumstances), game birds, children (in uniform), burglars, if caught on the premises, and Irishmen, if suspected of being terrorists and providing the appropriate warnings had been given, were outside. Danny simply presented the picture of a small boy, in short trousers, sitting on a bale of scratchy straw, listening. The question was implicit. *You said I had a clear understanding that killing was wrong. Are you sure?*

Danny found it harder to talk about the break-up of his parents' marriage.

'What went wrong?' Tom asked.

'The farm was failing. Basically, once he'd done all the field draining and fence building and that sort of thing, he lost interest. Didn't have a feeling for the chickens, for keeping them alive, I suppose. And the whole point about battery hens is they're supposed to stay alive, for a couple of years anyway. You can't wring their necks, and then complain they're not laying. And he was a bit above the hard grind of working on a farm. Or he thought he was. He was an officer and a gentleman, so obviously if he was a farmer he had to be a gentleman farmer – what other sort could he possibly be? He spent a lot of time in the lounge bar of the Red Lion, buying rounds of drinks with money he didn't have. The locals saw him coming. They were laughing at him behind his back, overcharging him . . .'

'This is your grandmother again.'

A smile. 'That's right. She didn't like to see my mother dragging herself about doing really hard physical work, while he propped up the bar. Quite right too.'

'You listened to the women talking?'

'Yes.'

'What did you feel?'

'Angry. Because in my mind he could do no wrong.'

'In spite of the beatings?'

'They were my fault.'

Tom let a silence open up. 'So. Financial pressure.'

'Yes. And then my mother found a lump in her breast, and she had to have a mastectomy. I went to the hospital with Dad, but I had to stay outside in the car. I was there all by myself, splashing in puddles. He seemed to be gone years, and then he came back, and pointed to one of the windows. She'd dragged herself out of bed to see me. He said, "Look, there she is." And I waved like mad, but there were hundreds of windows. I didn't dare say I couldn't see her. Then, after she came out, things really went to pot. She just couldn't do it any more. They got this girl Fiona in to help, and he rallied round a bit, of course he did, but I don't think he had the slightest comprehension of what she was going through. One or two jokes when her hair fell out, that can't have helped. And one day I was walking across the field to the cowshed

126

– Dad's workshop – and I heard Fiona laughing. I don't know why I didn't walk straight in, but I didn't. I looked through the window, and there they were, on the bales of straw. Hard at it.'

'What did you do?'

'Went away.' A pause. 'You know, the awful thing is, I blamed my mother. That was the really bad time. And then he left. And, by a curious coincidence, so did Fiona.'

'How old were you?'

'Nine years and 362 days. It was three days before my birthday. I was sure he'd left me a birthday present somewhere. I ransacked the house, but of course he'd cleared everything out, all his drawers and cupboards were empty. And then I thought, He'll have left it in the cowshed. And as soon as I thought about it, it was so obvious that's what he'd do. So I went and searched there, and I found his binoculars. They were hanging up under an old coat, and I sort of convinced myself he'd hidden them there, that was the present, he'd left them for me, only he hadn't had time to wrap them. And I kept them round my neck all the time. Went to bed with them, everything. They were quite powerful: you could zoom in really close, see the hairs in somebody's nose if you wanted to. And they wouldn't know. I remember looking at my mother crossing the yard with buckets of feed, and her hands were red raw. She'd just come out of hospital after the third lot of chemotherapy, and she was feeling sick all the time, but . . . Bloody hens still had to be fed. I knew I ought to go down and help her, but I didn't. I turned the binoculars round, and then she was just a little beetle crawling across the yard.'

A silence. 'You still blamed her?'

'Yes.'

'Did you see your father again before the trial?'

'No. And I wouldn't have seen him then if the newspapers hadn't found him.'

'He came every day.'

'Shamed into it.'

'And he visited you at Long Garth.'

'Ego trip. My son at boarding school. The minute I tried to talk about anything, he got up and walked out. Well, I told you. I watched him from the bedroom window, striding away down the drive, fast as his legs could carry him.'

'What did you feel, watching him walk away like that?'

A flash of impatience. 'What do you think I felt?'

'I don't want to guess, Danny. I want you to tell me.'

'Nothing much. He'd walked out before, he was walking out again. That was what he did best.'

He looked drained.

'I think we should leave it there,' Tom said.

Probably not a good moment to leave it, but then no moment was going to be good. Whatever happened in these sessions Danny would be alone with it afterwards. Tom tried to imagine the room he was going back to.

On the pavement Danny hesitated, the light from two street lamps disputing his shadow. 'Right, then,' he said. 'Thursday.'

A brief, taut smile, and he was gone.

ELEVEN

At six, Tom gave up trying to sleep, pulled on a tracksuit and trainers, and let himself out of the house. The river was smooth as glass, but as the sun rose the wind sharpened, flicking the brown water into little skips and bursts of foam. He loved this: the smell of the sea on the dawn wind, the city, with its precipitous streets tumbling down the hillside, silent in the clear air.

He jogged past the empty warehouses in a capsule of his own noise: gasping breath, pulsing blood, pounding feet. He was thinking about Lauren: the messages he'd left on her answering machine, the cool voice that returned his calls. She'd decided it was over, and the fact that he hadn't jumped on a train and gone down to see her meant he thought so too.

She was coming home this weekend, and he was well aware it might be for the last time. He'd spent half the night thinking of ways of rescuing the situation. A long holiday? But she was about to start term, and he had to finish the book. Six months' trial separation? But they were separated already. They'd had all the time in the world to think. He stopped by one of the deserted quays, clinging to the rusting railings while he fought for breath. Far below the river sweated oil.

Back home, he showered, forced down two slices of toast, and set off for the station. Still preoccupied, he parked the car, bought a newspaper, located the right platform, paced up and down, all on automatic pilot, hardly aware of the sour smell of old smoke in the station, or the people hurrying past. And then, suddenly, he was here, inside his own body, his own life, this moment. He took a deep breath. The smell made him think that somewhere up there, trapped under the glass roof with its colony of golden-eyed pigeons, were the ghosts of steam trains of the past: diesel fumes, burning coke, wet coal, smoke clearing slowly from platforms, passengers emerging after long journeys with soot-smudged faces and red veins in the whites of their eyes.

Lauren was wearing a silver-grey trouser suit, and she was not in the least red-eyed. During the night he'd rehearsed countless ways in which she might say what he was convinced she was going to say. Blurt it out, right there on the station? No, not Lauren's style. Wait till evening, and tell him over dinner, drowning bad news in litres of red wine? Risking the inevitably uninhibited row that would follow? He should have known better. Lauren walked towards him along the platform, swinging two extremely large, and obviously empty, suitcases. She didn't need words at all.

Automatically, he tried to take the suitcases from her.

'No need,' she said, lifting them up and down to show how light they were.

They walked out of the station to the car. Lauren raised her face to the mizzle. 'Why is it always raining here?'

'It's raining everywhere.'

'Not everywhere. It was fine in London.'

She swung the suitcases on to the back seat, and got in beside him. The air in the car smelt cold, foisty and damp. When he switched the heater on, the windows misted over.

'You're taking a few things back with you then?'

She turned to him in the dingy light. 'Well, actually, Tom, it's a bit more than that. I don't think things are working out. For either of us. So I thought I'd – well, you know.'

'Move out.'

'Yes. I want a divorce.'

No point challenging Lauren with plain speaking. She was on for any amount of it.

'A divorce.' Somehow the word shocked him. He'd been thinking of separation, of . . . He didn't think she'd got that far.

'It's not working, Tom, is it?'

He might have insisted it was. As long as he claimed

the marriage was alive, she couldn't unilaterally declare it to be dead. 'No,' he said.

He flicked a lever up and water jetted on to the windscreen. Squeak, whine . . . whoosh. More water. Whoosh. 'Well, we can't sit here all day,' he said.

'Don't back out. You can't see.'

'It's okay. The heater'll work in a minute.'

But she got out, leant into the car through the back door and rubbed condensation off the rear window, her face, in profile, tight, preoccupied, exasperated. Everything about him was wrong at the moment. It was the only way she could get through it.

When he'd reversed safely, he said, 'Will you be going back tonight?' He could ask that quite calmly and coldly. None of it was real to him yet.

'No, I thought I'd stay over. If that's all right?'

'Be my guest.'

That helped both of them. They drove the rest of the way home in a satisfyingly irritated silence.

The silence didn't last. They owed it to their marriage to talk, and talk they did, endlessly, though not because there was anything left to say.

Dinner was in a Chinese restaurant, whose dark-red flock wallpaper made Tom feel he was trapped inside somebody's mysteriously fur-lined intestines. '*The* marriage', as they'd begun to call it, sat with them at the table. They ordered food, and picked at it, and a litre bottle of wine that they sank in record time.

'The thing is,' Lauren said, not quite steadily, 'I can't stand not being wanted. I know it's not your fault, I know you can't help it, it's not voluntary, I know that, and I'm not blaming you, I'm really, truly not blaming you, but I can't stand it. It's . . . I just feel completely and utterly humiliated. I feel as if I'm turning into this little dried-up shrivelled old woman –'

'You're not. You're beautiful.'

'But that's how it *feels*.'

'I'm sorry.' He spread his hands helplessly. 'I don't know what else to say, except it's my fault. It's not yours. I don't understand why it's happened any more than you do.'

'I can't go on.'

'No, I know you can't.' Silence. 'And I can't say, "Give it another six months, it'll get better," because . . . it's not like that. I don't know what else I can say.'

Back home, drinking the second bottle, they found plenty to say, both of them. Round and round, up and down. The fact was, Tom thought, in one of those moments of total clarity that characterize drunkenness, they actually needed to have a short, simple conversation, and they couldn't bring themselves to do it, because it seemed an insult to everything that had happened in the last ten years. So they kept burying and disinterring, and carrying out elaborate rambling inquests. At last, exhausted, in the early hours of the morning, they started a full-scale row, only to stop in the middle of it, slightly embarrassed, realizing they no longer knew each other well enough.

Then, they began to talk about the practical details of disentangling their lives. Would the house have to be sold? If so, how was the equity to be divided? Which pieces of furniture would Lauren want to take? There was something mildly indecent about this conversation, like talking about insurance policies when the person insured is still clinging to life. Nothing useful was said, but the mere fact of trying to grapple with these mundane matters made each of them believe – in Tom's case, for the first time – that it was going to happen.

It seemed ridiculous to share a bed after that, and, after ten years, equally ridiculous not to. Tom got undressed in the bathroom, but refused to hunt out his pyjamas. They'd always slept naked, and it would have seemed . . . stupid to do anything else now. But all the same, he went back into the bedroom feeling like a plucked chicken.

The cold air round his groin reminded him of the first horrible night in boarding school, two rows of little boys standing on the ends of their beds, in darkness, while Matron, a terrifying woman, bore down upon them, one by one, scooped their genitals up in a white cloth, and shone a torch in the folds of skin on either side. Searching for *Tinea cruris*, of course, but they hadn't known that. God knows what they'd thought was going on. He remembered it clearly: the cold, the dark, the circle of light, Matron's blurry face, bending down, the lines of pallid, frog-like little boys.

Sliding down the cool sheets, he realized that what had triggered the memory was not merely the embarrassment of nakedness in front of an unfriendly audience, but the sense of abandonment.

In the dark, sweating, he rooted towards her, blind as a mole, and she opened up to him, put her arms around his shoulders, pressed her face into his stringy hair. He lay, half on top of her, one hand clamped round her thin wrist, and she bore it, but inwardly, where it mattered, he felt her withdraw from him. More than anything else, this tolerance, this kindness, convinced him she meant what she said.

After a decent interval, she eased herself from under him, but it was a long time before he knew, from the evenness of her breathing, that she'd gone to sleep, and longer still before he managed to follow her.

The following morning he woke early. Sunlight streamed into the room through a gap in the pale-grey curtains. Lauren had kicked off the duvet during the night, and he lay looking at her, amazed by that cello-on-its-side flare of the hip, and the fuzz of fine golden down in the small of her back.

His cock was achingly hard. Well timed, old son, he thought bitterly. Spot on.

Breakfast was coffee and toast, eaten standing up in the kitchen, followed, on Lauren's side, by two hours of packing. She'd bring a van for the pictures and the furniture, she said. She'd ring him early next week to agree on a time. As to what she'd be taking, they could sort that out later, over the phone.

He was relieved they weren't going to haggle about it now. In fact, he was determined not to haggle at all, though he'd seen enough of other people's divorces to know how corrosive the process of separation can be. He sat in the living room, hearing her move around upstairs. It seemed unreal. At last the suitcases were filled and locked and their straps buckled. He carried them down to the hall.

Already the house felt depleted, though nothing had gone except the contents of Lauren's wardrobe and a chest of drawers. One or two ornaments. He looked at a circle in the dust on the mantelpiece in their bedroom, and tried to remember what had been there. They were fading already, the details of their life together.

They had two hours to fill in before her train left. Nothing seemed right. In the end they spent the time, as they had often done on Sunday mornings, at the Quayside market.

The pubs were open. People crowded the pavements, bare-armed, sweating, boisterous. The air was hot and dusty, freshened by the merest hint of a breeze coming off the Tyne. The market had changed in the years they'd been coming here, become more of a tourist attraction, less obviously a place where items that fell off the backs of lorries changed hands with no questions asked. Once there'd been touts, posted at either end of the aisles, to warn stallholders of approaching policemen.

A crowd had gathered near the bridge, and they drifted in that direction. A young lad, twelve or thirteen years old, wearing only a pair of stone-coloured shorts and sneakers without socks, stood hugging himself. Little wizened nipples like berries on his chest. Tom noticed his shape most of all: small for his age, short-necked, short-waisted, pigeon-chested, that curious concertinaed look you used to see on girl gymnasts from the Eastern bloc. He was staring round the ring of people. Beside him, on the ground, lay a sack and a heap of rusty chains.

Suddenly, with a great scrape and rattle, a man with a bald head and tattooed arms swept the chains off the ground and carried them round the circle of spectators, pressing them – bullying them, almost – to test the strength of the links. He wore his long, dirty-blond hair in a ponytail; a bare torso rose out of filthy jeans. Tattoos covered his body everywhere, every available inch. Above the sagging belt were the words PUSSY MAGNET in red and blue.

A few people, Lauren amongst them, drifted off, not liking the hectoring tone, but most stayed to watch. Something deeply unpleasant about this, Tom thought, nasty, though the boy, who, after all, was more than half naked, showed no signs of ill treatment, no lacerations, no bruises. He was skinny, but not undernourished, and seemed bored, or indifferent, rather than cowed. He stepped into the sack. His father – if it was his father – pulled it over his head and tied it. Then he began to wind the chains round the sack, padlocking them as he went, until boy and sack had been transformed into a mummy whose bandages were iron.

A small, thin woman began to beat a drum. The bundle convulsed, each end struggling to meet in the middle, like a chrysalis beginning to split. Tom almost expected to see yellow fluid oozing from the bag. More convulsions, grunts of effort, turning, writhing. The chains screeched on the flagstones. No progress, though, until suddenly, amidst a growing murmur of concern, the first chain fell away. The boy jackknifed, and then, in a single movement, stood up holding the last padlock above his head.

The crowd clapped, a grudging ripple of applause that seemed to infuriate the tattooed man. Grabbing the boy by the arm, he dragged him round the break-ing circle, thrusting a cap into people's faces, almost shaking the coppers out of them. Tom threw all his loose change into the cap, not because he was intimi-dated, but because he felt ashamed of having been present.

The performance had deepened his depression. He was glad to get away. He began searching for Lauren, pushing his way up and down the crowded aisles, looking for a pale, blonde head, thinking how strange it was that, for an hour or so longer, he still had the right to look for her. The market was no more than a quarter of a mile long, but he couldn't see her. Nothing could have happened to her. Still, there was a constriction in his throat, a fullness in his chest, and he began to shoulder his way roughly through the crowds. At last, forcing himself to stay calm, he climbed some steps and scanned the crowd, slowly and methodically, left to right and back again, and there she was. Not alone. Talking to somebody, a tall, dark-haired young man standing with his back to Tom. His head looked familiar, but it wasn't until he turned slightly that Tom recognized him. Danny Miller.

No reason why he shouldn't be here. He was a student: this was one of the few places students could afford to shop. He must have identified Lauren from her photograph on Tom's desk, and stopped to speak to her. No reason why he shouldn't. Yet the sight of them together made Tom uneasy.

It was odd, he thought. He'd spent hours watching every flicker of expression on Danny's face, noticing torn cuticles, clean nails, the size of his pupils, minute changes in the way he dressed and held himself. And somehow in the process he'd stopped seeing him. At any rate, stopped seeing what Lauren was seeing now. A quite exceptionally good-looking young man.

Danny had height, good looks, charm. Thirteen

years ago, watching him in the witness box, Tom had asked himself, How can so many things be right? With an uncomfortable sense of treading in his own footsteps, he asked it again now.

He set off through the crowds, wanting to get there quickly, hardly knowing whether he was worried about Lauren's safety (but what could possibly happen to her here?) or simply disconcerted by the sense of exposure that the sight of her and Danny together aroused in him.

He reached her in time to see Danny's back disappear into the crowd. 'Who was that?'

'The boy who tried to drown himself.' She was flushed. 'I'm glad I bumped into him. I was wondering what had happened.'

They stood facing each other. She pushed a strand of hair behind her ears in a gesture he was going to have to get used to not seeing. 'Well,' she said.

Somewhere a church clock chimed the hour.

'We ought to be getting back,' he said, sparing her the need to say it.

They set off, letting the crowds separate them, grateful to be able to postpone, even for a few minutes, the need to say goodbye.

TWELVE

Tom had been living alone, except at weekends, for more than a year now. There was no reason why Lauren's deciding to get a divorce should make the house seem larger, but it did. He came down next morning to a living room that had expanded to the size of St Pancras Station. Pieces of furniture stood with their backs to the wall, watching him. One false move out of you, mate, they seemed to say, and we're off too.

He spent the morning trying, and failing, to work. Then he rang his mother, arranged to have supper with her, and over the meal told her the news, which came as no surprise, and left, just after ten o'clock, feeling . . . brutal. He'd cancelled the future.

When he got back, the house seemed to have become emptier. Ridiculous; he was used to coming home to an empty house. Walking round it – since there was clearly no point in going to bed – he discovered that some rooms were worse than others.

The bedroom, surprisingly, was tolerable. He simply switched to sleeping on Lauren's side. The kitchen was very bad. Even sitting in her chair, he was aware of the noise of his own eating, biting, chewing, swallowing, and he couldn't stand it. Like feeding time at the zoo. After the first morning he ate breakfast standing up, or walking round the garden, and had supper upstairs on a tray.

The computer screen unnerved him. The winking cursor was both too demanding, and not demanding enough. It could be ignored, as a patient sitting in the chair beside his desk could never have been ignored. He began to search for things to do to take him out of the house. He arranged to see Bernard Greene, Danny's old headmaster, and he made a list of interviews he needed to do with kids on the Youth Violence Project.

Ryan Price was the first name on the list. Making the appointment wasn't easy, because Ryan's mother wasn't on the phone, but keeping it was worse. He couldn't take a taxi because no taxi driver would go on to the estate. He couldn't park outside the house because the car would be stolen or torched by the time he got back, and the bus dropped you off on a corner that had one of the highest rates of muggings in mainland Britain. In the end he drove to the nearest GP's surgery, left the car in one of their secure parking spaces and walked the rest of the way.

He turned the corner into Belford Street, and saw

a police car pulled up on the kerb outside Ryan's house. Two policemen were getting out. The older one nudged his companion. 'Hey up, here comes the silver streak.' A reference to a time, two years earlier, when Tom had got done for speeding. The police never tired of the joke.

'Which one are you after?' the older one asked.

Tom shrugged and spread his hands.

'Well, if it's Robbie and Craig, you can't have 'em.'

Big beer belly on him, the older one, but no swagger, no aggression. The younger one, all feet and Adam's apple, was already peering into the living-room window.

Jean Price, a thin woman whose eight-month pregnancy barely showed, leapt up from a sofa laden with half-naked children, and ran to the window. 'What do yous lot think you're doing? Looking in at my window at half-past eight in the sodding morning?'

'Howay, Jean. Open the door.'

'You're enough to give anybody a heart attack, you.'

'C'mon, love. We're only doing our job.'

She knew she had no choice. The door opened. 'Only doing your job. Pair of bloody piss artists.'

'We've come for Robbie and Craig, Jean. They were supposed to be in court yesterday, weren't they?'

'And what's that got to do with me? It's not up to

me to get them into bloody court, know what I mean?' She looked over their shoulders at Tom, whom she regarded as an ally, of sorts. 'Can't you tell them?'

They followed her into the living room, an almost bare room with an unguarded electric fire. The children, in vests and little else, stared at the policemen with big eyes.

'Don't get yourself upset, Jean,' beer belly said.

'Don't get meself upset? I thought you were doing it.' She raised a finger. 'Them lads is fifteen and sixteen years. They're old enough to get theirselves off to court, know what I mean? They get letters from their solicitors reminding them. They can read.' She bent to pick up a child's shoe, but couldn't settle. 'If they don't want to go to court, that's up to them.'

Beer belly went to the foot of the stairs and yelled, 'Craig? Robbie? Come on down now.'

'Hands off cocks, on socks,' the younger one said.

'Eeh, will you listen at the language in front of them bairns?' She was talking to Tom now. 'What the bloody hell am I supposed to do? I was sat in court when I was nine months pregnant with her. Here, this one. She was bloody near born in court, her.'

Beer belly started up the stairs.

'Oh, make yourself at home,' Jean yelled after him. She turned back to Tom. 'This is harassment, this is. I've got eight kids, I'm a single parent, I don't need this.' She was struggling to put on a little girl's socks as she spoke, but her hands shook so badly she had to give up. 'I'm on tablets for me nerves, as it is. Anybody with kids this hour, they're getting them off to school, know what I mean?' She rounded on the police. 'If you waited half an hour I'd be sat here with a cup of tea, know what I mean? Might even've give you one.'

Craig and Robbie tumbled into the room. Immediately Jean started slapping them hard about their heads and shoulders. 'I haven't half got summat to tell them about yous, pair of bleeding poofs.' The police towered over her. 'Barging in here half-past eight in the pissing morning.' She turned to Tom. 'I'm not telling you a word of a lie, I've bled every month of this pregnancy. I'm losing now.'

'Then let's get you to the doctor,' Tom said.

'What's the point of that? He'd only put me in hospital. Where can I go into hospital?' She pointed to the children, who stared solemnly back at her. 'You know as well as I do, if that lot got took into care, I'd never get 'em back.'

Robbie finished pulling his trainers on and stood up.

'Right, then, are we off?' beer belly said. 'Can we give you a lift to the station, Jean?'

'Oh marvellous, that is. How many do you want me to bring? All six of 'em, or just the baby?'

He shrugged, and pushed Craig out of the door. Jean and Tom watched from the window as the boys got into the back of the car, the younger policeman putting a hand on their heads to protect them.

At the last moment Jean ran to the door. 'Mind you ring for a solicitor now, our Robbie. And Craig? Don't you go blabbing your mouth.'

The car drove off. Jean, still fuming, went back to dressing the little girl. 'Oldest trick in the book, that. Get me to leave the bairns in on their own, then ring the social services. Bingo, whole bloody lot in care. That's one thing nobody can say about me,' she added, ramming a shoe on. 'They're not neglected, and I don't go out and leave 'em on their own.'

'Nobody thinks you neglect them, Jean.'

'Hmm.' She was slightly mollified. A second later she grinned. 'Here, have you seen me stood sideways?' She demonstrated her almost flat stomach. 'Me mam says, "By heck, our Jean, where the hell are you keeping it?"'

Tom said, 'Look, I know this is a bad time –'

'No, you're all right, love.'

He was never sure how Jean thought he fitted into their lives. Her manner with him was always slightly flirtatious, she seemed to feel he was on her side, but she didn't seem to see it as a professional connection. 'I was hoping I could see Ryan.'

'Oh God, yes, so you were. Do you know, I'm that frazzled I don't know what I'm doing half the time.' She yelled up the stairs, 'Ryan!'

A second later Ryan appeared, bleary-eyed and yawning. 'Have the police gone?'

'Yeah.'

'What did they want?'

'Not you. They come to take Robbie and Craig to court.'

'Pair of poofs.'

'Hey you, they're your brothers.'

Ryan was rubbing his thigh. 'Our Craig give us a dead leg.'

'Ryan,' Tom said firmly, 'suppose we go in the kitchen and have a chat?'

A shrug. 'Yeah, all right.'

Perhaps it was his own depression, but this morning the view from planet Ryan seemed even bleaker than usual. School: waste of time. He'd been suspended anyway. What did he feel about that? 'Not bothered.' Wasn't it a good idea to get some qualifications? 'Not bothered.' Like most of Jean's children, he was not stupid, and now and then burst into connected speech. Teachers lived in their own cosy little world. They wouldn't last five minutes outside the classroom. Why wouldn't they? They knew nowt. They thought it was marvellous if somebody passed their exams and got on to one of the slave-labour schemes. £1.99 an hour. Tom tried to get him to talk about the security guard whom he and his mates had thrown down an escalator in the Metro Centre. 'Them bastard security guards are always giving us hassle.' But the guard was still on crutches, wasn't he? How did Ryan feel about that? 'Not bothered.' At moments like this, Tom thought, you felt these were really rotten kids, and that there was very little else to be said about them.

He walked back to his car. Every house left vacant here was stripped of fireplaces, bathroom fittings, pipes, roof tiles, and set on fire, either for fun or because the owners, despairing of selling or letting the property, paid children to do it. At the corner of the street there was a skip full of burning rubbish. A knot of children, on the other side of it, shimmered in the heat, like reflections in water.

That evening he phoned Martha, and said one word.

'Detox?'

'Right.'

They met in a bar in Northumberland Street, and ordered a bottle of wine.

'So what's been happening?' she asked.

'Oh, nothing horrendous. I was interviewing Ryan Price, and somehow – I don't know – it just got to me.'

' "Not bothered," ' she said in Ryan's monotone.

'That's right. You know he threw a security guard down an escalator? Well, him and the gang.'

'Yeah, figures. He spent six weeks in traction when he was a kid. Robbie threw *him* downstairs.'

'Hmm. Nice to see family traditions being carried on.' He took a sip of wine. 'You know, I looked at that estate, and I thought, if . . .' A quick glance round the bar, then he continued in a lower voice. 'If Ian had done what he did there, there wouldn't have been nearly the same uproar.'

'No,' she said. 'Because that's *them*. But as soon as you get a kid committing murder in rural England – or small-town America, same thing – you're attacking the . . . I don't know, the myth – the moral heartland. And the press have hysterics. Do you know they're still after Ian now, they're still nosing around?'

'I thought nobody knew he was out?'

'Well, officially nobody does.' She shook her head. 'They know everything, Tom.'

'But they don't know the name?'

'No, well, my God, I hope they don't.' She rested her steepled fingers against her lip. 'Ian says you're going to see other people.'

'Yes. Well, only one so far. I've arranged to see his old headmaster, Bernard Greene.'

'You will be careful, won't you?'

'You mean I mustn't say the new name, even there?'

'That's right.'

Tom sat back, smiling. 'You're sure this isn't just Home Office paranoia?'

'You've never had the tabloids on your tail.'

They finished the bottle and, at his insistence, ordered another. He could talk to her about Lauren, but he needed a few drinks before he did it.

'So what went wrong?' she asked, playing with the stem of her glass.

'Sex,' he said. 'In the end I wasn't much use.'

'Brewer's droop?'

It was amazing what Martha could come out with and still sound sympathetic. '*No*. Ovulation-prediction-kit droop.'

'You were trying for a baby?'

'Yes. And yes, I do know how irresponsible that sounds. But we were all right when we started trying. That's what I can't understand – it's all gone down the plughole in such a short time. And I keep looking back, and you know if you're not careful the present starts to destroy the past, because all the time I remember as happy I think, well it can't have been like that. There must've been something wrong and I was missing it.'

Getting pregnant had become an obsession, he said, knowing this was, in effect, blaming Lauren, and not liking himself for it. But everything he said was true, or as close to the truth as he could get. He'd felt used, and he'd withdrawn, not consciously, not deliberately, but . . .

'You can see why she was desperate, though, can't you? How old is she?'

'Thirty-six.'

'Yes, well, I'm thirty-four and I think that's bad enough. It's not the same for men, is it?' Martha's usual cheerful expression had soured. 'Never send to know for whom the clock ticks. Because it doesn't bloody well tick for thee.'

'I didn't design the equipment. If I had, I'd have included a permanently inflated tube.'

'Hey, be good that, wouldn't it?'

'Yeah. You could strap it to your thigh when it wasn't required.'

'Well, *you* could.' She hesitated. 'Did you ever try with anybody else?'

'You mean —'

'Try. Have a go. I mean it's all very well saying it's ovulation-prediction-kit droop, but I don't see how you can know if you haven't tried with somebody else.'

'Thanks, Martha. That's a great help.' He brooded for a moment. 'No, I didn't try,' he said at last. 'I was married.'

'Well, you're free now.'

If that had been said by anybody else, he'd have thought it was a come-on. But not Martha. It wasn't that she was unattractive — in fact at one point, when they first started working together, he'd found her worryingly attractive — but they'd gone too far down the path of friendship to be able to turn back and choose the other route. Making love to Martha would be like pulling on an old, warm, well-trusted sweater on a cold dark night. She deserved better than that, and so did he.

Outside the bar, they kissed goodnight and he set off to walk home, hoping that the combination of fresh air, exercise and far too much to drink would enable him to get to sleep.

The nights were bad. He found himself regularly

standing at the window, at two or three or four a.m., staring up and down the street. Once he thought he'd identified a fellow insomniac. A bedroom light, nine or ten doors down, kept going on and off, and he took some comfort from the presence of a fellow sufferer. Over the following nights he identified a pattern and realized the light was coming from a lamp wired up to a timing device. He felt the loss of this unknown companion as a distinct twinge of pain, and wondered that anything so trivial could make itself felt amidst the general misery.

Tonight, though, he fell into a deep sleep and woke refreshed. He lay and watched sunlight creeping over the carpet towards the bed. And this morning, instead of forcing himself upstairs to his attic workroom, as he did every day, he was driving to Long Garth.

Somewhere inside his head, Martha's voice said, 'You're free now.'

As he went down to breakfast, he thought about it. Being free didn't stop the pain, or the bewilderment, or the sense of failure, but it was a new and equally valid perspective on his situation, and it demanded attention.

THIRTEEN

Long Garth, the secure unit where Danny had spent seven years of his life – what was left of his childhood and all his adolescence – lay in a fold of green country-side beneath Brimham Rocks. Having arrived too early for his appointment, Tom drove up to see the rocks, huge granite boulders left strewn across the moorside as the last Ice Age retreated, some grouped together, some isolated. One block of granite was so finely balanced on top of another that it swayed in the slightest breeze.

Tom watched the moving rock, then looked down over the moorside, listening to the distant bleats of sheep that came and went as random as wind chimes. He could see Long Garth from here, a low building surrounded by playing fields, with the blue oblong of a swimming pool set a little to one side. Once Long Garth had been part of a much larger institution for adolescents in trouble with the law, but that had been closed down. Fashions change: the extreme isolation of the setting was now thought unsuitable for the rehabilitation of young offenders, but the secure unit remained. Twenty-four adolescents – all boys – behind a sixteen-foot-high perimeter fence.

Tom had never met Bernard Greene before. He'd written to the Home Office three times, in the first year after Danny's conviction, emphasizing how important it was that Danny should receive professional help rather than be subjected to mere containment, and each time he'd received the same bland reply. Danny had settled in well. Progress towards his eventual rehabilitation was being made. But Tom had heard from other sources that there was no provision for psychotherapy at Long Garth, and Danny confirmed this. Instead he'd received an eccentric, old-fashioned form of public-school education: large grounds, well-equipped classrooms, small classes, firm moral teaching, an emphasis on the role of games in the training of character. No wonder his father had approved.

Cloud cuckoo land, Tom would have said. No relevance at all to the treatment of a severely disturbed child, except that Danny *had* flourished here, for a time at least.

Bernard Greene lived outside the grounds, down a narrow lane that ran parallel with the perimeter fence. A wisteria covered the front of the house, its leaves rustling in the breeze. It had the effect of making the house seem alive, a sheltered space within the garden, but not separate from it. The leaves were beginning to turn. He couldn't imagine what this place would be like in winter: bare moors, icy winds and, on the skyline, those precariously balanced rocks.

The door was opened by a large woman, one hand still wearing a red-and-white-striped oven mitt. 'Dr Seymour?' she asked. 'Come on in. My husband's expecting you.' She stood smiling at him, her face shining with perspiration or steam, a rather jolly, unathletic games mistress in a girls' school.

He stepped into the hall. A bowl of roses stood on the hall table, the silver reflected in the polished wood. Even the fallen petals, little pink and yellow gondolas, seemed to be part of the arrangement. Smells of lavender and lemon. Yet Mrs Greene had made no effort with her own appearance. A shapeless dress splodged with blue cabbage roses covered a body she'd clearly decided to forget about. Thin, grey-brown hair, clean and neatly combed, but not styled. She'd given up.

She opened a door on the right. 'Dr Seymour to see you, dear.'

Bernard Greene was hovering just inside the door, waiting to come forward and offer a cool, dry hand. Immediately Tom felt antagonistic. Why had he not got up and answered the door himself? Why leave his wife to come all the way from the kitchen, like a servant, when he was nearer? Greene's whole appearance was elegant, self-contained, slightly boyish. Crisp grey curls, intensely blue eyes – so intense Tom suspected tinted contact lenses, though he couldn't see the rim – sun-tanned skin, forthright manner, an erect almost military bearing. The contrast with his wife was startling. He looked about twenty years younger.

Well, perhaps he was younger. Tom sat down in the chair indicated: a chintz-covered armchair at the opposite side of the fireplace from Greene. An elaborate arrangement of dried flowers hid the empty grate. On his left was a grand piano, covered with photographs of two young girls, in their school uniforms, on horseback, playing in the garden, giggling on the edge of a swimming pool.

'My girls,' Greene said, as if his wife had played no part in their production. 'Away on a school trip at the moment, so the place seems very quiet. Do you have children?'

'No,' Tom said. He thought it an odd question to ask at the start of a professional interview, almost as if Greene were trying to undermine any claims to competence in dealing with adolescents Tom might be about to make. 'Thank you for seeing me at such short notice.'

'Not at all. Only too pleased to help, though I don't know there's much I can tell you. Are you treating him?'

'Not exactly. He wants to . . . to talk to somebody about, well, about the past, what happened, why it happened. I don't know whether you remember – I was called as an expert witness at the trial.'

'So you know most of it already?'

'Some of it.'

Mrs Greene said, 'I'm surprised –' then thought better of whatever it was she'd been going to say. 'Would you like some tea?'

Greene glanced at Tom.

'I'd love some.'

When she'd gone, Tom asked, 'Has Danny been in touch since he left?'

'No. He wrote once or twice, but that's all.'

'Did you expect him to? I mean, *do* they come back?'

'Some. I thought Danny might.'

'Why do you think he didn't?'

'I don't know. If you're seeing him, you could ask him.' After a short silence, he went on, 'I think he felt . . . let down. I'm afraid I did more or less promise he'd be allowed to serve his sentence here, at least until he'd turned nineteen. Because there was a prece- dent for that, you see. Another boy did that, and . . . He was actually released from here, but in Danny's case the Home Office decided to transfer him to a top-security prison. So he left.' A flash of bitterness. 'And I've no doubt it took them six months to undo all the good we'd done in seven years.'

'Can I start by going right back to the beginning? What was your first impression?'

'We were gobsmacked,' Mrs Greene said, coming back in with the tray. 'Do you remember?' she asked her husband.

'Yes,' he said.

'We were in the waiting room when the warder came in with him. He was so small. And then when we got him back here and saw him beside all the other boys –'

'He was the youngest by three years,' Greene said.

'All you could do that night was put him to bed,' Mrs Greene said. 'He was totally worn out. Oh, and he was terrified of wetting the bed, and he wouldn't let himself go to sleep, he tried to stay awake, and of course he did wet it. He used to hate doing it. I think he hated anything he couldn't control.'

'My wife taught him French,' Greene said.

This was a dismissal and she took it as such. When the door closed behind her, Greene said, 'Does he know you're here?'

'Yes. I wouldn't come without his knowing, though having said that I shan't be repeating anything you say.'

'How is he?'

'Pretty good. I think it's a hopeful sign that he wants to . . . come to terms with what happened.'

An indulgent smile. 'Come to terms? I wonder if that's possible. What could it possibly mean to come to terms with the fact that you killed somebody?'

'All right. He wants to set the record straight.'

'You mean find somebody else to blame? It's best left. You know the first thing I do with any boy coming to this school? I say to him: this is the first day of the rest of your life. I don't care what you've done. I don't even want to know what you've done. All I'm interested in is the way you behave now. The moment you walk through that gate you start living forwards.'

Greene positively glittered with conviction. For the first time Tom saw that this man might be charismatic, particularly if you were young and troubled and you wanted to forget.

'So nobody ever spoke to Danny about the murder?'

'No.'

'And he didn't attempt to raise it?'

'No. You've got to remember he was still saying he hadn't done it. In Danny's mind there was nothing to talk about.'

'He's mentioned an English teacher.'

'What did he say?'

A surprisingly sharp question. 'Nothing much. Just that he was very good. Angus . . . ?'

'MacDonald. Yes, he was good. And very well meaning.'

Tom smiled. 'That's generally said about people who create havoc.'

'No, I didn't mean that. He was . . . totally committed. Good degree, good references, but no experience, no . . . sense of danger, I was going to say, but that's not the right word.' Greene groped. 'He ended up poddling about in things he wasn't qualified to deal with.'

'He got Danny writing about the murder?'

'As I understood it, he asked him to write about his childhood. I don't think even Angus would've –'

'And you disapproved?'

'I didn't know. If I had, I'd certainly have warned Angus to steer clear.'

'So how did you find out?'

'Danny. He came to see me. Though I knew something was wrong before that, because his behaviour had deteriorated.'

'In what way?'

'He attacked another boy.'

'Badly?'

Greene shrugged. 'Depends on your standards. He tried to stab him with a screwdriver, but the boy wasn't injured. As I'm sure you realize, assaults here are fairly frequent. But, of course, after that it all came out. By "all" I mean the sort of probing Angus had been doing.'

Greene sat back, bright-eyed, nursing his teacup, waiting for the next question, giving nothing.

'Was Danny a good swimmer?'

Surprise. 'Excellent. He used to swim for the school.'

'Against?'

'Other young offenders' institutions.'

'Was he allowed out?'

'Under strict supervision, yes. As were the other two boys who were serving life sentences. There was never any preferential treatment.'

Tom was left wondering why Greene supposed he thought it possible that there might have been. 'But you'd have to make some sort of – I wouldn't say preferential – *special* arrangements for his education, surely? I mean he was doing three A levels. What proportion of the boys here do that?'

Greene smiled. '0.001 per cent. Yes, of course we made special arrangements, just as we would've done if a boy had been profoundly deaf, or blind, or . . . Fairness doesn't mean you treat boys in exactly the same way. It means you devote equal attention to their needs.'

Greene had been on the defensive ever since Tom had mentioned Angus MacDonald. 'Was he rewarding to teach?'

Greene's expression . . . softened? No, not softened – kindled. 'He was one of the brightest boys I've ever taught. I used to teach at Manchester Grammar School, and of course we got some very bright lads there. When I came here I told myself I didn't miss it. Seeing these boys come on . . . it's another sort of satisfaction. But for a teacher there's nothing quite like feeding a mind that can take everything you give it, and come up asking for more. So yes, he was rewarding.'

'Did all the staff like him?'

The enthusiasm faded. 'Of course not. We're a small community. There are always going to be tensions in a place like this.'

'Would you say the school succeeded with him?'

'Yes, I would. I don't know to what extent the experience of prison was destructive, but when he left here he was . . . Yes, well, I will say it. In many ways a fine young man.' He glanced at the clock. 'And now I'm afraid . . .' His hands closed over the arms of his chair. 'Oh, you haven't finished your tea. No, don't rush. My wife'll see you out.'

Tom shook hands, thanked him again, then walked across to the window and watched him go. A curious bustling, tripping walk, as if the movement came from the knee rather than the hip. He became aware that Mrs Greene had come into the room behind him, and was watching him watch her husband. He turned, and picked up the tray. 'Shall I carry this?'

'That's very kind of you. Would you like another cup?'

She was being jolly hockey sticks again, but the eyes were dark and shrewd.

'Yes, I think I could manage another.'

He followed her into the kitchen. It had a good feel to it, this room: dressers rather than fitted units, a minimum of modern gadgets, old, well-cared-for utensils lying around, a scarred chopping block, rows of sharp knives. A bunch of Michaelmas daisies in a square green-and-white vase stood on the central table. Tom sat down while she moved around filling the kettle and setting out clean mugs. 'Can't be doing with cups, can you? If it's worth having at all, I always want a lot.'

A pot simmered on the cooker. 'I wish I could offer you a more appetizing smell, but I'm afraid it's still at the scraping-off-scum stage.'

She sat down, wrapped her pound-of-sausages fingers round the mug and blinked at him. 'Well,' she said, when he still didn't speak. 'Danny.'

'You taught him French. Was he good?'

She tubed her mouth. 'Yeah. He was bright, good memory, good mimic. There's not a lot else to learning a language at the early stages.'

'How old was he when you first started teaching him?'

'Eleven. The same age he would have been if he'd' – an unreadable flicker of expression – 'followed a more normal path.'

'Did you like him?'

An abrasive laugh. 'Oh, that's a dangerous question to ask round here. I didn't ask myself if I liked him. That wasn't the point.'

'No, but you could ask yourself now.'

'And come up with a straight yes or no?'

He smiled. 'Whatever you come up with I'd like to hear.'

'Danny was a bottomless pit. He wanted other people to fill him, only in the process the other people ended up drained. Some people were . . . I don't know, mesmerized by the process, and so they kept going back for more. Or rather they kept going back to give more.'

'You say they were mesmerized by the process?'

'Or by him. This place is full of people wanting to help, that's why we're here. And most of the time you can't help, so when you meet somebody like Danny who makes you feel you *are* helping, well . . . it's water in the desert. And he was very, very good at making people think they were helping.'

'He was probably desperate to be helped.'

'Yes, I'm sure.'

Tom was feeling his way forward. 'Do you think Mr Greene ended up drained?'

'No.' Very definite. 'My husband is . . . well, devoted to the boys, as I'm sure you saw, but on the personal level he can be . . . quite impervious, as well.'

Tom found himself trying to translate that into terms that might have been used by somebody less admiring (presumably she *was* admiring) of Greene and his work, but the only phrases he could come up with were swingeing.

'Bernard has a great gift. He can look at somebody and see the best person they could be, and somehow he manages to believe that person into existence. But the downside is that he's actually rather naïve about the way people are now. He's not shrewd. In fact, I think he rather despises shrewdness, he thinks it's cynicism.'

Tom was puzzled, and he took a moment to work out why. It was because he'd expected more resentment from this woman who was treated like a housemaid, expected to run and answer the door, sent off to make the tea, then dismissed, abruptly, although she'd taught Danny and might well have had something to contribute. But now, looking round the kitchen, he saw that this, not the study, was the power centre. Seen from this changed perspective, the study looked rather like a playpen.

'And this suspension of disbelief worked with Danny?'

'You tell me.'

Tom hesitated. 'Well,' he said. 'They let him out.'

He saw her smile. Tom didn't want to make the same mistake he'd made with Greene, closing down the conversation by focusing on a topic that produced a defensive reaction, so he asked the most open-ended question he could think of. 'What was it like dealing with him?'

Silence: the silence of having too much to say. 'I'm sure my husband told you he got no preferential treatment?'

'He did, yes.'

'The whole school was reorganized round him. Everybody thought he was bright, just talking to him, you could tell, but they did a battery of tests and realized he was very bright, so that meant an academic course. A lot of the time he was taught on his own, one to one. Most of the time here we're coping with illiteracy.'

'But that was inevitable, wasn't it?'

She nodded. 'Yes. And of course he was a child. People responded to him as a child. His housemother fell in love with him. I don't think that's putting it too strongly. No children of her own, and suddenly there's this beautiful little boy. He *was* beautiful.'

'But it didn't stop there, did it? I think you're . . . well, I think you're implying Danny worked the system.'

'Like otters swim. I think most of the time he was so good, nobody saw him doing it. In any relationship, but especially with an adult, he had to be in control. And – well, I think this is why he wasn't spotted – it wasn't control as a way of getting something, it was control for its own sake. Little things . . . it's a rule the boys don't call staff by their first names. Bernard's a great believer in keeping a certain distance, he thinks it's a mistake to start coming across as somebody's best mate. Danny used everybody's first name. And of course it didn't matter. Except. Another rule: you're not supposed to be alone with them. If you're teaching one to one – and everybody who taught Danny did – the door's supposed to be left open. Either that, or you do it in a corner of the library. With Danny the doors were closed. Not because anything . . . wrong was happening. It wasn't. But he'd be telling them something, he'd be confiding in them, he didn't want anybody else to hear, and they'd be flattered, they'd think: This is great, we're making progress. I'm the one who's broken through. And you see the really devilish thing? Danny wasn't breaking the rules. They were. He was very, very good at getting people to step across that invisible border. Lambs to the slaughter.'

'And one Aberdeen Angus bull.'

She looked surprised, but recovered quickly. 'Yes.'

'Did he do all this to women as well?'

'He did it to everybody.'

'Including Mr Greene?'

'Yes. That's when I first noticed him doing it. I don't suppose you . . . no, you wouldn't. My husband has a, well, a distinctive walk. Danny started imitating it. And there he was, bustling round the school like a miniature headmaster, it was . . . very funny to watch, and I think most people thought it was a good thing. Bit of hero-worship.' She paused. 'I didn't like it.'

'And where did Angus fit into all this?'

'Oh, he came much later. Danny was fifteen.'

A short silence. 'But the same thing?'

'Plus.'

A long silence. Tom said, 'Did he imitate Angus?'

'The accent. Angus was very Scottish.'

'And a good teacher?'

'Very. Though whether he was suited to this sort of work . . .' She seemed to come to a decision. 'Danny started mimicking him, anyway that's what Angus thought, and he cracked down on Danny pretty hard. He'd no experience with disturbed kids, he treated them as a normal class. Little sprog plays up. Crack down. But you can't do that here. To any of them, but especially not Danny. You see, all the other kids were on a points system. The more points for good behaviour, the sooner they got out. But not Danny.'

'Danny wasn't going anywhere.'

'That's right. Life. He didn't know how long life was going to be, but he knew it was going to be a helluva long time, and he knew being a good boy in English lessons wasn't going to get him out of anything. So when Angus cracked down, Danny freaked out. Bounced himself off the walls, tried to break the windows, threw things, generally went berserk. And suddenly it wasn't a normal class.'

'What did Angus do?'

'Saw him afterwards. Alone.'

'With the door closed.'

'I shouldn't be at all surprised.'

'And then he got Danny writing about his childhood?'

'Yes. I don't think he was trying to get at the murder, though I don't know where else he thought it was leading.'

'You obviously think it was a bad idea.'

'Well, from Angus's point of view, yes. You do know Danny accused him of sexual abuse? He had to leave.'

'No, I didn't know.'

Tom was almost too surprised to speak, and the more he thought about it, the more baffled he became. Danny's silence might be explicable, but what about

Greene's? What about Martha's? There was no way this wouldn't be on the file. Unless . . . 'Was there an inquiry?'

'No. Angus was on a one-year contract. It all blew up towards the end of the summer term. He left a bit early.'

'With references?'

'That I can't tell you.'

'And the stabbing? Mr Greene said –'

'*Attempted* stabbing.' She shrugged. 'Incidents like that happen here all the time.'

'What caused it?'

'The other boy said, "Everybody knows you're MacDonald's bum boy."'

'So it was about Angus?'

'Yes.'

'Do you believe there was a sexual assault?'

She pursed her lips. 'There may have been a *relationship*. Not that I'm justifying it for a minute, but . . . Angus wasn't the only person to leave over Danny. I can think of another four.'

'Who had relationships?'

'No, no, just got over-involved. You'd be amazed how many people didn't believe Danny had killed that woman. When he tried to stab the boy in the woodwork class, the teacher who was taking the class was absolutely shattered. Not by the incident – by what he saw in Danny, because he was one of the ones who couldn't believe he was guilty. Danny didn't pick fights, you see. So it was easy for people to slip into thinking he wasn't violent. And this teacher said he thought, My God, there it is.'

The tea was cold. 'Would you like another?'

'I'm taking up a lot of your time.'

'Nothing's spoiling. I'll put the kettle on.'

She got up and began moving around. Tom watched her thinking that he still had no real idea what she felt about Danny. 'I'm interested in what you were saying about Danny's mimicry. If that's the right word.'

'No, it was more than that. He . . .' She groped for the right word. 'Borrowed other people's lives. He . . . it was almost as if he had no shape of his own, so he wrapped himself round other people. And what you got was a . . . a sort of composite person. He observed people, he knew a lot about them, and at the same time he didn't know anything because he was always looking at this mirror image. And of course everybody let him down, because you couldn't *not* let Danny down. Being a separate person was a betrayal. And then you got absolute rage. Angus had no idea what he was tangling with.'

'You really didn't like him, did you?'

A short laugh. 'I thought he was one of the most dangerous boys we've ever had through the school. Bernard thinks we transformed him. I don't think we even scratched the surface. Or, if anybody did, it was Angus, and look what happened to him.'

171

'Do you know what did happen to him?'

'Angus? He runs some sort of writers' centre. So he stayed in teaching, that's one good thing.'

'Do you think I could have the address?'

'Yeah, hang on a sec, I'll get it.'

He went to the patio doors and stood looking over the garden, while she turned over papers in a drawer. Green lawns, rose bushes, blue shadows creeping over the grass. Beyond the trees, the smooth, windowless walls of the secure unit, as disturbing, in the fading light, as a face without eyes.

'We used to live in there,' she said, coming back. 'Can you imagine? Bernard said it did the boys good to have a normal family living with them. I'm afraid I had to put my foot down, and point out that the normal family wasn't going to stay normal if we didn't get a bit of privacy.'

'It must get quite claustrophobic.'

'It certainly does.' She held out a piece of paper. 'Here you are. North Yorkshire. Somehow I always thought he'd go back to Scotland.'

He thanked her and shortly afterwards left. She stood at the door, watching him go, and then, as he started to reverse the car, came out into the drive.

'Be careful, won't you?' she said. And he knew she wasn't referring to the fading light and the long drive.

FOURTEEN

Towards evening it came on to rain. The river was a confusion of overlapping rings and bubbles, too turbulent to reflect the blackening sky. Tom looked back into the room. 'I've been to Long Garth.'

'Did you see Mr Greene?'

'Yes.'

Danny smiled. 'I won't ask what you thought of him.'

'More to the point, what did *you* think of him?'

'Idealistic. Naïve.' A slight pause. 'Vain.'

'No, I meant when you arrived. When you were eleven.'

'I admired him, I think. He was like my father. In some ways. Very upright, clean, organized. There was absolute clarity at that school, and it came from him. You knew what the rules were, what the rewards were, what the punishments were, and it was always the same, and it was the same for everybody. You felt safe. I know a lot of people would say the regime there was pretty inadequate. But . . . you've got to start with the basics. You can't do anything in a place like that unless people feel safe. And we did. We were supervised round the clock. You couldn't go to the lavatory on your own, you couldn't close your door, you weren't allowed to be alone with anybody, you couldn't go out . . . It was absolutely bloody terrible, I hated it, but it worked.'

'And you met Angus?'

Danny looked surprised. 'Did Greene talk about him?'

'His wife did.'

'Oh yes. Elspeth. She didn't like me very much.'

'Why do you think she didn't like you?'

'Not partial to murderers?'

Tom let the silence deepen round the attempted flippancy of that remark. Then, 'Tell me a bit more about Angus.'

'I don't know that there's much to tell.' He was staring at Tom, perhaps trying to work out how much he already knew. 'He was a brilliant teacher.'

'Tell me about his teaching methods, then. What did he ask you to write about?'

'Usual stuff. A Storm at Sea. Masses of purple prose. And then one day he said, "Write about your grand-dad," and I wrote about the day my grandfather died.' Danny was reaching for another cigarette. 'I hadn't thought about it for years. He came into the kitchen talking about rabbits, thousands of them, he said, all over the top field, and there were drops of sweat on top of his bald head, grey, like dirty rain. And by midnight he was dead.'

'Of?'

'Pneumonia. Old man's friend.'

Danny seemed to have ground to a halt. Tom said, 'What else did you write about?'

A smile. '"My Pet".'

'Duke.'

'Yes. He was a bull mastiff, and he was kept chained up in the paddock by the side of the house. He used to watch the geese walk past on their way to the pond. One year he got one, just before Christmas. My grandmother said he'd watched them getting fatter. Quite old, smelly, ropes of saliva hanging from his jaws.'

'Did you love him?'

A blank look. 'I don't know.'

'Why was he kept chained?'

'Because Dad liked the idea of a powerful dog, but he didn't want the grind of training it. Like a lot of things about Dad, it was all show. And when he left home he left the dog behind.' He laughed. 'I think I was more shocked by that than his leaving me behind. Anyway, the dog was too big for my mother to cope with. My grandmother felt sorry for him and took him for a walk, and he dragged her through a bed of nettles. So he was given to a man who ran a scrap-metal yard. I used to go and see him in the school lunch hour, and there were notices all over the place.

"Beware of the Dog." There was a little kennel, too small for him to get into, and a bowl with no water in it. I told the other kids it was my dog and they didn't believe me. I went up and put my arms round him, and he stank. He was hot, he was slobbery, he was a horrible dog. I started to cry.'

'And that's what you wrote about?'

'Yes, and then the battery hens, and the pigs on the next farm. And in the end Angus said, "But I can't see the people." And of course he was right. No bloody way was I doing the people.'

'So how did he get you on to that?'

'He said, "Does your father use an electric razor?" And I said, "No," and he said, "Tell me about your father shaving." Well, that was always a time of enormous tension, because he didn't shave in the mornings if he was going to be on the farm all day, he shaved in the evenings before he went out. I'd be sitting with my mother in the living room on this leather sofa we had. If you were in short trousers the backs of your legs stuck to the seat, and when you stood up you really yelped. And my mother would be sitting in the armchair, pleating her skirt. On and on, making pleats, smoothing them out, making them again, and . . . not saying anything. And there'd be this bluthering and spluthering from the kitchen. He always got ready at the kitchen sink, almost as if he was trying to start a row. Because, you know, because he was going to the pub, and he was going to be spending money we didn't have, buying rounds for people who laughed at him behind his back. And there'd be this . . . tension.'

'Did they fight? I mean, did he hit her?'

'No, he hit me. He hit me to get at her.'

'So Angus was pressing on some raw spots.'

'Oh, it was dynamite. I mean, I'd totally blocked off the past. I didn't have any explanation for why I was in the secure unit. I was just there. I wasn't there because I'd done anything wrong. I believed my own story.'

'So why did you go on writing about the past? You could've stopped.'

Danny shifted in his chair. 'I think . . .' A sigh. 'I think I got addicted to the . . . intensity of it.'

'Did you feel it was dangerous?'

'God, *yes*. What the fuck did he think he was doing? Because you look at what he did, he took somebody with hypothermia, and put them next to a blazing hot fire. As soon as the feeling starts to come back, they scream their bloody heads off.'

'Yeah, I can see that. But then, the other thing you don't do with hypothermia is to leave people in the snow.'

'No, I know. No, I know it had to be done. And then he fell in love with me, and that didn't help.'

'When did you realize he was in love with you?'

'Quite late. I'm not sure I knew at all till after I'd left. If you mean when did I realize he wanted to fuck me, about five minutes after we met.'

'And he made love to you?'

'Yes.'

'How on earth did you manage that? You were supervised every minute of the day, locked in at night . . .'

'Well, he was doing the supervising, wasn't he?'

'And how long did this go on?'

'Two months? Not long.'

'Do you remember how it started?'

'I was walking past the window of his room, the room where he taught, and I tapped on the glass. He was sitting at the desk, marking books, and he waved to me to come in. And we talked. And that was all we did. But we were alone, and it was an absolute rule that we shouldn't be, and we both knew that. So there was this casual conversation going on, totally innocent, and at the same time . . . And then he had to go to a meeting, and that was that. Except he knew I'd tap on the window again, and I knew that when I did he'd wave to me to come in.' Danny smiled. 'It was all so bloody repressed you wouldn't believe. Talk about Jane Austen. And it went on like that for quite a long time. And then one day I brushed against him, deliberately of course . . .' He shrugged.

'But then the headmaster found out?'

Danny looked surprised, almost as if he'd forgotten how the affair ended. 'Yes, that's right.'

'And Angus lost his job.'

'Yes.'

'Did you tell the headmaster?'

'No, I told another teacher. She told him.'

'And there was no inquiry?'

'Nobody wanted one. Angus certainly didn't.'

'And that meant no more digging into the past?'

'Yes. Till now.'

Tom took the hint. 'All right,' he said. 'Your father had just left home and you were searching for the present you thought he must've left for you, and you found his binoculars.'

'And more or less went to bed with them for the next three months.'

'You also said you looked at your mother through the wrong end and she was tiny like a beetle and you didn't have to feel sorry for her. Did you feel sorry? It implies there was a problem.'

'Well, yes. It would've been a hard life for a woman, at the best of times, but she'd had a mastectomy. She'd lost her hair. She'd lost her husband. For Christ's sake. That Christmas she got one of the neighbours to kill the geese, and she sat in the shed till midnight plucking them. I went in, and the draught from the door made all the feathers rise up, and they take ages to settle. And when you looked at them every one of them had a little plug of blood at the end of the spine. I tried pulling some of them out, but of course I got bored, and she says, "It's all right, son. You go to bed." It was freezing in the shed. And the skin was this horrible dingy yellow, pimply, cold.' He pulled a face. 'I hated her because I couldn't help her.'

The word 'hate' seemed to liberate him. 'I hated her because she couldn't keep him. I hated her for being ill and miserable and bald and ugly and old. I hated the way her nose went red when she cried. And at the same time I was frightened she was going to die. Only even that was mixed because at the back of my mind there was a fantasy: if she dies he'll have to come and get me.'

'And it was just the two of you?'

'Yes, till the cancer came back and she had to have another mastectomy. And then my grandparents came and lived with us. I don't know how she'd have managed otherwise.'

'And then your grandfather died.'

'Yeah, babbling on about rabbits, poor old sod. Gran went back home. She couldn't do anything – she was ill herself. I think – I'm not sure – I think there was a bit of a breach. I think she blamed my mother for Granddad dying like that. He was doing too much, trying to help, and he couldn't, his heart was too bad.'

'It sounds as if there was a lot of blaming going on.'

'Oh, a tremendous amount.'

'How did you react to all this?'

'Went off the rails. Let me see, what was I doing? Starting fires. Once in my bedroom, I think that was the worst time.'

'How did it feel?'

'Marvellous. Fantastic. My mother said when she

came into the room I was staring at the fire, not doing anything, not trying to put it out. And that was awful for her, because then she felt she couldn't leave me, and she had to leave me. She'd got a job cleaning, by this time. The farm was up for sale, but it wasn't selling. She sold all the stock and lived on social security, Dad never sent a penny. And she got this little job, cash in hand, and she used to run all the way there and all the way back, and every time she turned the corner she fully expected to see the place on fire. Then I burnt the barn down. And there was one other little fire in the shed. The rest of it was all outside. But that was with other kids. We lit a fire once that took four fire engines hours to put out.'

'Did you watch?'

'Yes.'

'How did you feel?'

'Powerful.'

'The opposite of being hung up on a peg.'

A sour smile. 'Yeah.'

'And what did you do the rest of the time?'

'Moped about. Nicked off school. Stole.'

'On your own?'

'No, there was a gang of us. Except I think . . . I don't know.'

'No, go on.'

'I think they were more normal than me. I mean, we used to play at being the SAS behind enemy lines, and we'd be completely lost in it, the way kids are, but then the game would stop for them, and they'd go and do something else. I was inside the game all the time. And then I'd go to call for somebody and he'd come to the door, and say, "I can't play out today. Me nanna's coming to tea." And I'm like, What does he mean his nanna's coming to tea? We're the fucking SAS. I was inside the game all the time. I'd be lying in bed at night listening to Mum and Gran downstairs and they were enemy civilians.'

'And the fire-setting and the stealing?'

'Part of the game. Setting fire to enemy buildings. Living off the land.'

Any moment now he was going to claim that Lizzie's death was collateral damage. 'Who did you steal from?'

'My mother. Shops. Eventually houses.'

'With the gang?'

'Sometimes. Everybody nicked sweets from shops.'

'And stealing from houses?'

He hesitated. 'No, that was just me. It wasn't about money, though I did need it. I don't know . . . I liked being in the houses. Being there, breathing the air, leaving all these invisible traces all over the carpet. I liked the idea that when they came back they wouldn't know.' He shrugged. 'It's hard to explain. Nothing in the house could do anything.'

'The house was helpless?'

'Yeah – something like that.'

'Did your mother know?'

'She knew about the shops, because I got caught. The newsagent caught me. She had to go to the police station. And then the headmistress wanted to see her, I was playing truant, and then social services got involved. And that was worse than the police. She wasn't used to anything like that. And she did what somebody like her would do. She talked to the vicar, and he got me into the church choir. Oh yes,' he added, noticing Tom's expression. 'In the middle of all this, I became a choir boy. Only I stole from the boys in the choir, and the vicar came to the house, and said he couldn't have me in the choir any more. Not fair to the other boys. And that was it, she cracked.' He was stubbing a cigarette out as he spoke, grinding it flat. 'After the vicar had gone,' he said, at last, deliberately, crumbling fibres of tobacco between his fingers, 'she took the belt to me. The other thing he left behind. I thought, You can't do this. She lashed out, shouting, screaming, she looked so ugly, and I suddenly thought, *No*. And I caught the end of the belt, and wrapped it round my wrist. And then again. I swung her round and round, and then I let go and she crashed into the wall and slid down it. Her wig was all lopsided. She looked at me and I looked at her, and . . .' A deep breath. 'I ran out of the house. I didn't go back till nearly midnight.'

'What were you feeling?'

'Exhilarated.'

'Where did you go?'

'Nowhere. Just walked.'

He sat looking down at his hands, unwilling or unable to say more.

Tom broke the silence. 'How long before Lizzie's death was this?'

Danny looked up with an expression of mild surprise. 'Do you know I never realized? It was the day before.'

FIFTEEN

Lauren rang to ask when it would be convenient for her to come and collect her pictures and some pieces of furniture. 'Never,' he wanted to say, but stopped himself in time.

'Which pieces?' he asked, grudging and suspicious. He didn't want or mean to sound like that, but the idea of a van drawing up outside and men carrying away part of his home was unpleasant, to say the least. And, when he first heard her voice, there'd been a second of hope. He'd thought she just might say, 'Look, let's not do anything in a hurry. Let's give it a few more months.' Instead, there was this crisp, cool, businesslike request for a date and time.

'The hall table. The sofas in the living room, the balloon-backed chair, the chest of drawers in the bedroom.'

All hers. All entirely reasonable.

When he remained silent, she said, 'The hall table was a present from my father. I hadn't even met you.'

'No, no, of course it's yours. And the rest.' Take the lot, he wanted to add, take everything. At the same time he had an uncomfortably clear picture of himself grappling with the removal men on the steps. He'd lived with those things for years. They were part of him.

'So when would it be convenient?'

Never. 'Thursday.' And that word: 'convenient', he thought. He hated it. It was a non-word. Like going on talking about 'discomfort' when the patient's screaming with pain. 'About ten o'clock? Or is that too early?'

'More like one o'clock. I'm driving up.'

That raised the prospect of food. Drink. He didn't know whether she wanted that or not. Well, he could offer. She could say no. He didn't want to give her the opportunity of saying no. 'All right.'

He wanted to say something else, but then he heard a man's voice in the background, and her voice answering, muffled, because she'd put her hand over the receiver. 'Look, I've got to go,' she said, in a breathless rush. 'One o'clock, Thursday. Okay?'

No. 'Yes, all right. See you then.'

After she rang off he spent some time trying to convince himself that the voice in the background had belonged to his father-in-law, then wandered round the house, dreading the coming invasion. He looked at her paintings. Three of them in the living room, all attempts to capture that peculiar quality of the light on the river in early morning and evening, especially when the tide was out. The most successful was almost abstract: a blend of brown and silver-grey, with the ribs of the submerged boat showing above the water as the tide turned.

His favourite among these paintings was the sunset scene, for no better reason than that he'd been there when she painted it. Late one afternoon they'd taken a picnic and gone out to the estuary, and as the sun sank she set up her easel and started work.

Black bars of cloud across the horizon, but the water was calm, luminous, reflecting the last light of the sky. He settled down with a book, ostensibly reading, but in fact watching Lauren. She became a different person when she painted, opening a can of beer, laughing when the foam squirted into her face, barefoot, an old pair of his jeans tightly belted round her waist. Lauren was beautiful, and elegant, but she was not, except when painting, graceful. She was too self-conscious; none of her movements was exactly the right move-ment. Except at times like this, stepping back from the canvas, moving forward, dabbing, stepping back, dabbing again . . . Speeded up, she'd have looked like a hummingbird. 'It needs something in the foreground,' she said. 'You'll do.' So, carrying the book, he went and stood where she indicated. 'Put the book down, for God's sake. You look like Wordsworth.' She held his shoulders, manipulating him into the right pos-ition. He smelt Chanel 19, which he didn't find sexy, and turpentine, which he did – very. 'There.' A satisfied nod, and she went back to the easel. Looking out of the corner of his eye, he could just see her eyes above the canvas, contemplating him as a problem in light and shade, and beneath it, her bare feet doing their never-ending dance in the dirt.

Almost the worst thing about the last week had been the way in which the snag in his present life ran back into the past and unravelled it. Because they were splitting up, it was easy to believe they'd never really been happy. When he tried to visualize Lauren painting the estuary, the image was changed by the fact that she had left him. The slim figure in the baggy jeans became doubly insubstantial, as if her recording of that sunset over the river had been no more than the first stage of her saying goodbye. Holiday snaps: the need to record a place that you already know will live on only in your memory. In his memory she shifted from one foot to another, raised a can of beer to her lips, streaked paint through her hair, smelt of turps, but she was already dwindling. What this painting gave him, when he looked at it again, was reassurance. She'd painted the river because she loved it, and, grasping the reality of that love, not vaguely, not as a general proposition, but precisely, in the particular strokes of her brush, he was able to go on believing that she had also, once, loved him.

It helped, it soothed him, but on Thursday the paintings would go.

SIXTEEN

Four days after that conversation with Lauren, Tom found himself standing in a small railway station on the edge of the Yorkshire moors, watching his departing train dwindle to a doubtful wink of light in the far distance. After it had gone there was silence, except for the click of the railway lines contracting after the day's hot sun, and somewhere, in the far distance, a peewit crying.

On the phone, Angus had sounded brisk and efficient, his Scottish accent less pronounced than Danny's mimicry had led Tom to expect. No point driving, he said. The Scarsdale Writers' Centre was at the end of a mile-long track so potholed that only a Land Rover could manage it. And anyway it would be no trouble to meet him at the station.

Trouble or not, there was nobody here. Tom put his overnight bag down, and sat on a bench beneath a poster advertising the delights of Whitby, and another proclaiming the 24-hour availability of the Samaritans.

He was beginning to wonder how he should set about calling a taxi when he heard the click of high heels, and looked up to see a woman with long orange hair, trailing clouds of diaphanous fabric behind her.

'Are you Tom Seymour?'

He admitted that he was.

'Rowena Moody.' She announced her name as people do who expect it to be known, though it meant nothing to him. 'I'm one of the tutors on this week's course,' she added, the drawl of dissolute grandeur drying to a schoolmistressy snap, as she realized the 'Oh' of recognition would not be forthcoming. 'There's a bit of a flap on at the moment. This is the night we have an outside reader, and Angus was hoping to have . . .' Her voice sank reverentially over a name that even Tom, who read no literary fiction, knew to be famous. 'I told him it wouldn't happen. He's not going to trail up here. As far as he's concerned, there's only a hole in the ground between London and Edinburgh.'

They were walking briskly towards the Land Rover. All those flying draperies were making Tom think of Isadora Duncan, but Rowena got herself safely behind the wheel and tucked the yards of silk chiffon around her.

They lurched forward across the car park and out of the station yard. It rapidly became clear that Rowena had no business behind the wheel of a Land Rover or any other vehicle. She was lethal. 'Oops,' she said at one point, jamming on the brakes and placing her left hand in Tom's groin to reinforce the operation of his seat belt. 'I didn't see him at all, did you?'

It was a relief to be out on the moors, where there were comparatively few cars, and the sheep saw her coming, and fled.

'So how do you know Angus?' she asked, in what passed for a quiet moment.

'I don't really. It's a sort of a friend-of-a-friend thing.' He should have come with a story prepared, since there could be no question of mentioning Danny.

'So you're not an aspiring writer?'

'No, I'm a psychologist. I do write, but nothing creative.' The sooner they got off this line of questioning the better. 'Do you often tutor for this course?'

It was her third time. She was happy to chat about the arrangement: fifteen aspiring writers cooped up for a week with two professional writers: an apprenticeship system.

'It becomes quite an emotional pressure-cooker – you'd be surprised. Some groups more than others, of course.'

'How's this one?'

'We haven't found the weirdo yet.'

'Does there have to be one?'

'If you're lucky. Two or three, if you're not.'

Perhaps Angus liked intense, enclosed communities. At any rate he seemed to have found himself another one, or a succession of them. 'Does Angus teach?'

'He's teaching on this one, but no, not usually. He and Jeremy run the place. Jeremy's his partner.'

There was a questioning note to her voice. He had an uncomfortable feeling that his sexual availability was being explored. 'I haven't met Jeremy either.'

'No, well, he's not here this week. I'm afraid it's a case of when the cat's away . . .' She wrinkled her nose with fastidious malice. 'I wouldn't care to claim the path to the tutors' cottage has remained entirely untrodden.'

Without signalling or slowing down, she turned left on to a potholed lane bordered on either side by drystone walls. A steep descent, taken at speed, brought them to a low farmhouse that seemed to have burrowed into the side of the hill to escape the winds that had deformed every tree. Even now, on a peaceful autumn evening, a gust snatched at him as he got out of the Land Rover. On a stormy night you must feel you were out at sea.

Rowena led him into the house. Red-tiled floors, a huge vase of hemlock casting shadows across a white-washed wall, a bowl of pebbles on a wooden chest. She swept into the kitchen and he followed. A tall, fair-haired young man was standing at one of the work surfaces, squeezing meat out of sausage skins into a bowl.

He looked up and raised his eyebrows. 'Couldn't get sausage meat, would you believe?'

'Don't let Angus see you,' Rowena murmured. 'I don't think I could cope with a cardiac arrest. Where is he, by the way?'

'In the office. Trying to find a replacement.'

'Oh, not still.'

Angus was on the phone. He raised his thumb in the air when he heard Rowena's voice, saying into the phone, 'No, absolutely not. Of course I'll come and get you, and you'll stay over, won't you? There's no point going back tonight.' He listened, said: 'Forty minutes? All right, then,' put the phone down, and punched the air with his clenched fist.

'Success?' Rowena asked.

'Lucy says she'll do it.'

'Oh, thank God. Perks things up a bit, you know, midweek,' she said, turning to Tom. 'Getting somebody else in. They're sick of us by then. Though I must say I think they'll find poor Lucy something of an anti-climax.'

'Well, sod their luck,' Angus said, sibilant, but stagily so. 'And you must be Tom.' A warm, dry, firm handclasp, and a hard stare. 'I'm afraid I've got to dash off, but we'll see each other later. As I expect you've gathered, it's been quite a day.' He was taking the Land Rover keys from Rowena as he spoke. 'Could you be a darling and tell them in the kitchen she's a vegetarian? Tell them not to make a fuss – just make sure there's plenty of salad.'

After he'd gone, Rowena pulled a face. 'It's always

like this. He sweet-talks people into making the commitment, but then they don't bloody well show up.'

The dining room had blackened beams, white walls and an ancient fireplace. Three tall windows overlooked the valley, which was now brimming with blue light, though the sun still shone on the distant hills. Tom sat next to Rowena. Angus and Lucy, a small, brown woman with a shy and sour expression, arrived late and sat opposite. The food was good and washed down with large quantities of wine.

'There's a kitty,' Rowena explained, 'but some of us bring our own as well.'

She spent the meal pointing out the course participants to him. There were two elderly ladies, sisters apparently, both widowed – one of them, after her husband's death, had moved three hundred miles to be closer to the other – and until this week they'd been inseparable. Now they sat at opposite ends of the table, each looking, since there was a striking resemblance between them, like the other's mirror image. Neither of them spoke to the people on either side.

'That's Angus, for you,' Rowena said. 'He always sees them individually, and he pokes and probes away till he finds out what makes them angry. Calls it the grit in the oyster. You find the anger, you find the voice. Well, what makes Nancy angry is that her father used to get pissed and beat her mother up, and her mother was an absolute saint who brought eight kids up on next to nothing. And what makes Poppy angry is anybody saying anything against her father, who was a marvellous man, never once the worse for drink in his entire life, despite being driven up the wall by a nagging wife. There's only two years between them – and they seem to have grown up on different planets. Angus persuaded Nancy to write about the father's drinking, and she read it aloud to the group. And Poppy got up and walked out. And they haven't spoken since.'

'Do you think it's just a tiff?'

'No, I don't. I think it'll take years. And you've got to ask yourself: what's the point? Really, what is the point? I mean, okay, it was quite a nice little piece, but frankly we are not dealing with the Katherine Mansfield and Virginia Woolf *de nos jours*.'

'Would it be all right if you were?'

She looked sharply at him. 'Good question. Dennis Potter said all writers have blood on their teeth.'

'Who's the man sitting next to Nancy?'

'That's our recovering alcoholic. Wants to learn to write so he can warn others against the demon drink. Don't let him get you on your own. He'll tell you all about the times he was incontinent. Next to him' – Rowena lowered her voice still further, he could feel her breath on his cheek – 'we have the groupies: Esme, Leah and – can't remember. Carrie. They're out of sorts – they were looking forward to this evening. A male literary lion. They're all right – a bit histrionic.' Rowena clearly didn't think this was a word that could ever be applied to her. 'Next one along's a lay preacher. God knows what he makes of it. And coming round this way you see four extremely good-looking young men, and they're all gay, which is nice for Angus, but rather tough on the groupies. Oh, and that very beautiful girl's called Anya. She's wasted on that lot.'

Tom nodded to his left. 'And these three?'

Distaste and incredulity mingled. 'I think they just want to write.'

By the end of the meal a good deal of wine had been drunk, and a row had broken out in the kitchen between two of the extremely good-looking young men. Lucy, clearly dreading the reading, had turned an alarming shade of grey.

'I hope somebody's thought of the likely side effects of all that wine and beans,' Rowena murmured, as she flowed through into the sitting room, glass in hand.

She sat in a rocking chair, a little way apart from the others, with an ashtray at her feet. Tom sat at one end of a sofa, next to another rocking chair that was clearly intended for Lucy. Esme, Leah and Carrie sat on the red sofa, facing the fireplace. The lay preacher, arms clamped tight against his sides, shared the beige sofa with three of the gay young men. The fourth, whom Tom had met in the kitchen, separated himself from his friends, and sat with dilated pupils, blowing smoke from his nostrils. The two elderly sisters, one conspicuously raw-eyed, the other glittering with defiance, also sat as far away from each other as possible. Angus took a chair by the fireplace, and set a bottle of wine down at his feet. The recovering alcoholic sat opposite him, pointing his nose at the bottle with the single-minded concentration of a gun dog. Lucy sat in the rocking chair, and swallowed twice. Angus poured her a glass of wine, though water would have been more to the point.

Angus looked around with a glint of amusement, and began to introduce the reader. Lucy blushed at the eulogistic praise delivered in a voice so ostentatiously well modulated that anything it said would have sounded insincere. Expecting a literary lion (male), obliged to make do with one small tabby cat (female), the groupies sank deeper into the sofa, a single, disgruntled heap.

Then Lucy began to read. She might have been a wonderful writer: short of snatching the book away from her and reading it yourself, it was impossible to tell. She read in a quick, anxious monotone, no eye contact, not even at the end of the first chapter. Within fifteen minutes the groupies were asleep, heads thrown back against the sofa cushions, mouths open, limbs sprawled in every direction, blowzy goddesses awaiting the judgement of a pathologically indecisive Paris.

Tom sat well forward on the sofa, looked interested, stifled a burp, tried not to laugh, dug his fingernails into the palms of his hands, became aware of the heaving sides of the lady next to him, glanced up and saw the same battle between good manners, boredom, flatulence and mass hysteria played out all around him, and hastily looked down again. By now the noise of tummy rumbles, burps and outright farts had left the realms of chamber music and reached symphonic heights, and the quick, monotonous voice ran on and on. Lucy hadn't glanced up once, though she must have been aware of suppressed giggles spreading round the room. Why didn't she bring it to a graceful close? Why had she selected such a long reading? He glanced sideways at the page, saw another chapter looming, and realized she was reading on because she was afraid to stop. A whickering snore from one of the sleeping beauties woke the others, who stared round them with expressions of lively interest. Tom followed the reading till the end of the chapter, and started to applaud. Everybody, relieved at the possibility of making some socially acceptable noise at last, clapped till their hands were sore. Lucy looked up, timidly, relieved to see it had all gone so much better than she had feared.

'Thank you,' said Angus. 'That was memorable.'

Questions followed. Surprisingly intense this session. Did Lucy have an agent? Did she use a computer? Write every day? Plan the book before she started?

No questions about her book, but then, to be fair, they hadn't heard much of it. And then, thank God, it was over, and everybody was free to drink, especially Lucy, who'd sipped water during dinner, but now got spectacularly drunk in record time.

'You think we're all mad, don't you?' Angus said, coming up to Tom with glass and bottle in his hands.

'Do you think we could talk now?'

Angus glanced round, and noticed the recovering alcoholic bearing down upon him. 'Definitely.'

He pushed open the patio doors, and they stepped out on to the lawn. They walked down towards the fence, their feet leaving scuff marks in the dew.

'He will keep telling people about crapping himself,' Angus said. 'There's something repulsively self-righteous about it all. St Sebastian and the arrows. St Catherine and the wheel. St Terence and the shitty pants.'

'I suppose he thinks the more he humiliates himself the less likely he is to drink again.'

'I'd drink to forget I'd done it.'

Despite what he said, Angus was less drunk than Tom had supposed. Either he'd been pacing himself rather more carefully than the ubiquitous bottle suggested, or his capacity was formidable.

Angus rested his arms on the fence. 'Do you think confession's the only route to redemption?'

'I'm tempted to say no, though I don't know what other route there could be.'

Angus shrugged. 'If you believe in redemption.'

'But you believe in the power to change, presumably?'

'Presumably.'

'And anyway,' Tom said, 'I thought you were rather in favour of raking up the past?'

'Oh, I am. For its own sake. I don't flatter myself it's got any therapeutic value. In fact the whole idea of writing as therapy makes me puke. It amuses me sometimes to think about the talking cure, and how it's become a whole bloody industry, and how little evidence there is that it does a scrap of good.'

'If you mean counselling, there's quite a bit of evidence that it's harmful, or can be. People who get counselling immediately after a traumatic event seem to do rather less well on average than those who don't.'

Angus looked surprised. Tom wasn't saying any of the expected things. 'Why?' he asked.

Tom shrugged. 'My guess would be that people are meant to go numb, and anything that interferes with that is . . . potentially dangerous. Equally, of course, the numbness eventually wears off.'

'And then talking helps?'

'It's one way of getting at the truth.'

'And that makes you feel better?'

'Not necessarily, no,' Tom said. 'It's valuable for its own sake.'

'Well, yes, I think we can agree on that.'

As far as the theory goes, Tom thought, remembering one sister's raw eyelids, the other's hectic cheeks.

'Of course we're not talking about "the truth", are we?' Angus said. 'We're talking about different, and quite often incompatible, versions of it.'

'I thought we were talking about Danny.'

A pause. The sound of sheep munching grass drifted up to them from the valley, while behind them bursts of laughter came from the lighted room.

'How is he?'

'Reasonably well. Finding it a bit hard to adjust.'

'How long's he been out?'

'About a year. He's a student. Reading English.'

A sound somewhere between a snort and a laugh. 'Well, he had a lot of talent.'

For some reason this remark filled Tom with antagonism. 'I expect he still does.'

'They'll all be spilling out in a moment,' Angus said. 'Shall we go further down?'

They scrambled over the wall, and began to walk down the hill, their shoes squeaking on the moist grass. Sheep raised their heads to watch them pass, but didn't bother to move away. The sound of voices and laughter came faintly here. They turned and looked back, and the white farmhouse, with its lighted windows, emphasized the shared isolation of the hillside.

'Does he know you're here?' Angus asked abruptly.

'No. I'll tell him the next time I see him. There's a general agreement that I can see whoever I want to see.'

'Will you give him my address?'

'Only if you want me to. Do you?'

'Oooh. Now there's a question.'

Angus's voice had changed. It was less consciously well modulated; his accent had thickened; there was a catch in his breath Tom hadn't noticed indoors. Perhaps he was asthmatic, and the night air was tightening his chest, or perhaps the silence, the watching sheep, the gulf of white light, had created another self.

'Yes, why not? He might be curious enough to find out what he did to me.'

'What *he* did to *you*?'

'Yes, I suppose it does sound odd. I was in my twenties, he was fifteen. Obviously it was my fault.' He smiled. 'Anyway, what does it matter? Water under the bridge.'

'I'd like to know what happened.'

'Why?'

Tom started on the obvious reply: because I think it'll help me to understand Danny, and found himself saying instead, 'Because I'm standing in your shoes, and I'm starting to think it's a dangerous place.'

'Don't be alone with him, then.'

'I've got to be. Anyway, I'm not worried about that.'

Angus nodded. 'Lucky you.'

'What went wrong?'

'I fell in love with him.' A pause, while Angus contemplated, with a moue of distaste, the banality of the statement: its lack of any protective coating of cynicism or self-mockery. 'Almost as soon as I met him. I wasn't the only one, though, it took various forms. I'm not saying it was always sexual. In fact it wasn't. But he was directly responsible for four people – that I know of – leaving that unit. And generally it was because they were over-involved, or jealous. I just accepted it. Not simply the fact that everybody was intensely involved with Danny, but the pretence that it wasn't happening. That all the kids were treated exactly alike. Like bloody hell they were.' He pulled himself up, dismayed by his own bitterness. 'Have you seen Greene?'

'Yes. And Mrs Greene.'

'Oh yes. Elspeth.'

'Did Greene know what you were doing with Danny?'

'Sexually?'

'I meant the writing.'

'No, he didn't, and he wouldn't have approved if he had. We were always told we didn't need to know anything about them, the past was irrelevant, their backgrounds were of no importance whatsoever. And these were kids with completely fragmented lives. I mean, Danny was brought up by his parents, but he was the exception. There were kids there who'd had

five or six foster placements in one year. Just at the
... real bog-level standard of who they were and
where they came from, they had no idea. And I
thought it was important, and I still think it's important, to help kids like that construct the narrative of
their own lives. And to help them put names to
emotions. You got the impression with a lot of them
that they had a kind of tension level, and they didn't
know whether it was pain, boredom, loneliness, un-
happiness, anger, bewilderment, because they didn't
know the names. They only knew it felt bloody awful,
and they relieved it by bopping somebody else over
the head. So I don't apologize for what I was doing.
It needed doing. And it wasn't therapy. It was supplying a basic piece of equipment that the rest of us take
for granted.'

'Did you like Danny?'

'You mean, apart from loving him?' He thought
for a moment. 'There was nothing to like. He was
incredibly charming, shallow, manipulative. I mean,
beyond belief. Control was an end in itself. And he
was shut down. You were dealing with about 10 per
cent of him. And not only that. He was only dealing
with 10 per cent of himself. And he had this very
bright, cold intelligence, and he was talented – which
was gold dust in there, believe me! And it seemed
such a tragedy, that he was . . . frozen like that.'

'So you decided you'd thaw him out?'

'No, that's not true. He decided. The sort of topics

I was giving him were standard English essay stuff. It was Danny who started pushing it. I did say things like, "Look, I can't see the people." But he took that and ran with it. He got closer and closer, until you could hear them breathing, and okay, it was dangerous, but let's not forget, it was also something that needed to happen.'

'Did you ever think you ought to stop?'

'Yes. He didn't want to stop.'

'Did you ever say, "Slow down"?'

'I didn't know how close we were. You've got to remember I didn't know anything about the background. He'd be describing a particular incident and I didn't know whether it was the day before the murder, or the year before.'

'You could have asked.'

'Not without pushing. I never mentioned the murder.'

'Did he write about the time his mother tried to beat him with his father's belt?'

'And he grabbed it and swung her round? Yes.'

'Did he write about Lizzie Parks?'

'Yes, I think that's what did it. The next day I was due to see him, and he didn't show up. And that Sunday evening after tea he went to Greene and said I'd molested him. Greene sent for me. He established that I'd spent x number of hours alone with Danny, and that was it. I was out. I left the next morning.'

'Why do you think he went to Greene?'

'Because he was frightened. He couldn't stop, he knew he was going to tell me about the murder, and that was a terrible thought. Because he'd never actually admitted it.'

'Isn't it possible he found the sex disturbing? He was only fifteen.'

'No.'

'How do you know?'

Angus turned to face him, a glimmer of amusement in his pale eyes. 'I'm going to tell you something about the sex that'll really shock you.'

'I doubt it, but go on.'

'There wasn't any. It never happened.'

Tom took a deep breath. 'You've shocked me.'

'He cut my head off.'

'Why didn't you insist on an inquiry?'

'I'd been alone with him. It was my word against his.'

'And you thought Greene would believe him?'

'Greene didn't want a scandal. Bad for Danny, bad for the school. Bad for Greene.' A moment's pause. 'How close are you to the murder?'

'Pretty close.'

Angus grinned, and began walking back up the hill, calling over his shoulder, 'Watch yourself.'

They parted at the door. Angus walked away along the corridor, wine glass in one hand, bottle in the other, not looking back. Tom had no desire to rejoin the party, and instead went upstairs where he was to sleep, for the first time since childhood, in a bunk bed. The lay preacher was already there, on his knees beside the bed, praying. Tom hadn't encountered this before either. He undressed quietly, and tiptoed off to the bathroom. A woman muffled in a tartan dressing gown – one of the group who unaccountably wanted to write – was already waiting in the corridor.

Tom asked whether she was enjoying the course.

'Do you know, I think I am. It's not what I expected, but Angus is a brilliant teacher.'

Tom lay awake for a long time in the narrow bunk bed, listening to the snores of the recovering alcoholic. One of the beautiful young men came in – the sausage-squeezer, whose name was Malcolm – and got undressed in a shaft of moonlight. The lay preacher got out of bed and started to pray again. They had five days of this, Tom thought, turning on his side. He was worn out after one evening.

He must have drifted off to sleep, because the screams confused him. Somewhere out there was a woman or child in pain, and he struggled to sit up. The others were already awake.

'Is it a woman?' the lay preacher asked.

'No, it's an animal,' said the recovering alcoholic.

'Can't be,' said Malcolm.

He got out of bed and reached for his dressing gown. Tom and the recovering alcoholic followed him downstairs – bare feet slapping on the cold tiles –

and through into the living room. Empty bottles, full ashtrays, an air of desolation. Somebody asleep on a sofa.

'Do you suppose the doors are alarmed?' Malcolm asked, pushing them open anyway. He strode off down the lawn, Tom following. Another scream cut the air. The hairs on the nape of Tom's neck rose. The lights went on in the tutors' cottage. Rowena, wearing a white négligé, came out on to the grass. Then Angus, draped in a sheet. They all stood and listened. Just as they were beginning to hope it was over, another scream tore the darkness.

Rowena, her drawling voice suddenly clear and cold, said, 'It's a rabbit. They do sound incredibly human.'

'Should we kill it?' the ex-alcoholic asked.

'No, it's coming from the other side of the valley,' Angus said. 'It'd be dead before we got there.'

'Christ.'

'Look,' Malcolm said, 'it's going to die, and there's nothing we can do about it. I'm going back to bed.'

He strode away up the lawn. Very sane and sensible, Tom thought, and yet, not. An hour ago there had been talk, laughter, companionship, lights, warmth, wine, food, and the screams had blown it all away. Each one of them stood there, shivering, condemned to the isolation of his own skin. How fragile it all is, he thought.

He felt Angus's hand heavy on his shoulder. 'Back

to bed,' he said, pushing Tom gently towards the house. 'There'll be a fox along soon.'

'Will we see you at breakfast?' Rowena asked.

'No, I don't think so,' Tom said, over another scream. 'I have to get back.'

SEVENTEEN

He'd forgotten that he was dependent on other people for transport. It was ten o'clock before anybody was free to drive him to the station, and then the train was late and he missed his connection in York. He'd intended to be in the house when Lauren arrived, though she had a key. She wouldn't be waiting in the street.

They were between Durham and Newcastle when his mobile rang. 'Tom, is that you?'

'Yes.'

'Look, I'm in the house. You remember I was coming back to collect some of my stuff? You said today would be all right.'

He could tell from her voice she was worried. 'What's wrong?'

'You know the boy you pulled out of the river? He's here. He said he had an appointment. I thought you must just have gone round to the shops, so I let him in.'

'Are you all right?'

'I think so.'

'What's he doing?'

'Walking up and down.'

Her voice dropped to a whisper, difficult to hear. The reception wasn't good anyway. The next thing he heard was: 'I've tried talking to him, but it's no use.'

All along the carriage people were standing up and reaching for their bags. In another minute they'd be queuing in the aisle. The train terminated here.

'Look, leave him alone. We're coming into New-castle now. I can be there in twenty minutes.'

If he got off now before everybody else. If there was no queue at the taxi rank. He grabbed his bag and pushed his way to the door, where he waited, jittery with impatience, for the light to turn green. Then he ran, weaving between hurrying people, and burst out of the station to reach the taxi rank before anyone else.

Once inside the cab, he drummed his fingers on his bag, ignoring the driver's attempts at conversation. The traffic was reasonable, and the journey took fif-teen minutes.

Outside the house, he stuffed a handful of coins into the driver's hand and waved away the change.

He let himself in as quietly as he could, and stood in the hall, listening. A murmur of voices from the kitchen. At the foot of the stairs were two suitcases, one of them open, half full of small objects wrapped in newspaper. Stacks of paintings wrapped in brown paper rested against the wall. Through the open door of the living room he saw grey ghost squares on the walls where the pictures had hung. Some pieces of furniture had been pulled out and placed in the centre of the room. He felt a pang of grief, for the end of his life with Lauren, for the joint person they'd been. And into this intensely private trauma had come Danny, whose voice he could hear downstairs. He hadn't known till now how little he trusted Danny, though there was an irrational element in his anxiety. The screams of the snared rabbit lingered in his mind, and he hadn't managed to get back to sleep.

He walked slowly downstairs. Through the banisters, he could see Danny's feet in black-and-white trainers. Nothing else. A floorboard creaked, and he heard Lauren say, with a rush of relief in her voice: 'That'll be Tom now.'

She stood up as he came into the room. He would never know how they would have greeted each other if they'd been alone. She came across the kitchen and offered him her cheek to kiss. He saw the moistness on her upper lip where pinpricks of sweat had broken through the make-up, and there was a peppery smell that came from her body, not from deodorant or scent.

'Hello, darling. Sorry I'm late.' He turned to Danny. 'And Ian, this is a surprise.'

'I think I may have got the wrong day.'

Even as he offered Tom the easy way out, Danny looked pleadingly at him. Lauren was standing with her back to the kitchen table, her thin arms crossed over her chest. Her lower teeth nibbled at her upper lip. Tom felt as if he were seeing her for the first time. It was extraordinarily distracting: this feeling of a pivotal moment in his own life being played out in front of an uninvited audience. Danny's hands were twisted in his lap, a knot of white knuckles, like worms.

'Well, never mind, you're here now, though I'm afraid I can't manage the full hour. But I've got a few minutes.'

He took Danny into his consulting room. All the way there he was aware of Danny noticing dust squares where paintings had been, a table pulled away from the wall, gaps in the book shelves, the remaining books collapsed on to each other in slack heaps. Danny's face showed nothing but embarrassment, and yet Tom was aware of a line being crossed. Danny was inside, now.

Perhaps the anxiety got into Tom's voice. He said sharply, as soon as they sat down: 'Now, then, Danny, what's this about?'

'You've seen the news?'

'No, I haven't.' This was obviously not the moment to mention his meeting with Angus. 'What's the matter?'

Briefly, Danny explained. Two little boys, eleven and twelve years old, had been charged with the murder of an old woman. Two newspapers, and the late-night news on the BBC, had run 'think pieces' on the story. What is happening to our children? etc. Since the Kelsey murder was sub judice, and therefore not available for public debate, they'd illustrated their points with references to Danny's crime. Even more seriously they'd used his school photograph.

'It's going to open up again,' Danny said, his voice strangled with misery and fear. Already he'd seen on television all the things that had happened to him: fists beating on the sides of a police van, shouted threats, the blaze of publicity, nowhere to run, nowhere to hide.

'What exactly did they do?'

Danny denied any knowledge of this. He'd switched off the television as soon as he saw his photograph and gone straight to bed, half expecting his landlady to bang on the door and throw him out.

'I really don't think anybody would recognize you from that photograph,' Tom said. 'I know I didn't.'

'Some people would,' Danny insisted. 'I'm like you, Tom. I remember voices, I remember the way people move, but you've got to remember there really are people who never forget a face.'

A frisson of unease. That was an entirely accurate description of the way Tom's memory worked, and yet he couldn't recall any conversation in which he and Danny had talked about the different ways people recall the past.

It was also the first time Danny had called him Tom. This was the wrong moment to object, and anyway Tom had one or two adult patients who used his first name. It probably didn't matter too much either way. And yet it jarred.

'Have you phoned Martha?' he asked.

'I can't get hold of her. I keep trying.'

'I'll have a go too. And I'll try my secretary.'

He put through a call. Martha had been in to the Family Welfare Centre, but had just left, saying she was going away. She hadn't said for how long. Tom tried her mobile, but it wasn't switched on. Turning back to Danny, he said: 'Look, we will get her. Don't worry.'

'I always knew it wouldn't work. There're too many people out there wanting to get me.'

Tom settled down to listen to him, aware of Lauren in the background pulling a piece of furniture across the floor. Danny was most afraid, not of violence, nor even of having his false identity blown – though these were real fears – but of the raking up of memories. Every newspaper, every news bulletin. On the Metro, coming to see Tom, he'd heard people talking about the crime, and he thought he'd heard the name: Danny Miller. It had disturbed him so much that he got off the train at the next station and found a seat in another carriage. 'I don't want to know what they did. I'm thinking about Lizzie all the time anyway. I don't need this.'

'Do you want to stop our sessions for a few weeks till this is over?'

No, he didn't. In fact the exact opposite: he wanted to press on faster. 'I've got to get it out now,' he said. 'Before all this muddies the water.'

Tom could see the sense in this. He didn't believe Danny would walk past the news-stands and not buy a paper. He didn't believe he'd switch off the television whenever the case was mentioned, and such was the urgency of his desire to make sense of what he'd done, and so insurmountable the barriers preventing him from doing it, that there might well be seepage from the reported facts of the crime into his memory of Lizzie's murder.

The doorbell rang, and he heard Lauren go to answer it. Two male voices. He wanted to be able to see what was happening.

'All right,' he said, standing up. 'Look, you can see things are pretty impossible here at the moment. Can you come back this evening? Say about seven?'

Danny moistened his lips. 'Yes, all right.'

'There really is no danger, Danny.'

Danny shook his head. 'You didn't see them banging on the van. They can't get those two, but they can get me.'

Tom showed Danny out, then stood with his back to the door, bracing himself. Lauren was in the living room, sitting on the arm of the remaining sofa. This perching, this waiting to take off, irritated him. Why on earth couldn't she sit down?

He started to say: 'How long do you think it'll take?' but stopped halfway through, startled by the booming of his voice. Of course, the removal of furniture and paintings had altered the acoustics. It was like speaking into a phone, when somebody on another floor has forgotten to put the extension down.

She answered the incomplete question. 'Not long. About half an hour.'

Her voice sounded different too. He realized he was going to remember this echo-chamber conversation as the sound of his divorce. Two people who used to love each other mouthing banalities in an empty box.

'Would you like a drink?' he asked, meaning, I'd like a drink.

She hesitated. 'Yes, why not?'

He uncorked a bottle and came upstairs with two glasses. All these simple actions were so heavily invested with memories that he felt like a priest celebrating Mass. He searched for some way of making the handing over of a glass of red wine seem less sacramental, and failed to find it. 'Well,' he said, struggling to keep the irony out of his voice, and failing again. 'Cheers.'

'Who is that boy?' she asked, turning away from him and walking over to the window.

'Ian Wilkinson.'

She looked puzzled. 'I know the face.'

'Of course you do. You met him on the Quayside.'

'No, before that.'

Tom shrugged, but his heartbeat quickened. Danny was right. Lauren was strongly visual, far more so than most people, and something about Danny's face tugged at her memory. She'd recognize him from the school photograph.

And if she did, others would.

To distract her, he said, 'You know the most horrifying thing about all this? Only a few weeks ago we were trying for a baby.'

'Yes, I've thought a lot about that. Thank God it didn't work.'

That for him, and perhaps for her too, was the moment when it ended. They were strangers now, not close enough to be antagonistic, trying to sort out the best way of disentangling their financial arrangements.

'Will you want to sell?' she asked.

'I don't think so. I might let out the top floor. It wouldn't need much doing to make it self-contained. And I suppose the lawyers'll sort out what to do about your share of the equity.'

'I don't want a long wrangle.'

'Nor me. It's more a question of what they want.'

They chatted for half an hour, finding it increasingly difficult to keep a conversation going. The topic he most wanted to raise – had she got somebody else? –

was taboo. It wasn't his business any more, though that didn't stop him speculating. He scoured her face and body for signs of sexual fulfilment, but she looked as she always did, elegantly turned out, cool.

He wondered how it felt to be leaving the house for the last time. She'd loved it when they first moved in. All those months spent painting the river in every possible light, and then she'd exhausted whatever it was she'd found here. After that, he thought, she hadn't liked the house much. On one wet day recently, peering through mizzled windows at the swollen river, she'd said they might as well live on a bloody boat.

It was a relief when the removal men came in and said they'd finished.

She stood up at once and looked at him. 'Well, Tom, do you think we can wish each other luck?'

For a moment the anger almost choked him. You're going, he thought, and you want me to wish you luck? But then he folded her stiffly in his arms, and patted her shoulders. He was surprised by his reaction. She felt wrong against him. The skin of his chest and arms was saying, Wrong body, so that, in the end, seeing her off for the last time, closing the door afterwards, he was able to feel that this parting was, to some extent, his decision.

A few minutes later, pouring himself another glass of wine, he realized that only a slight change of perspective was needed to make it all his decision. He could have gone to London with her and e-mailed chapters of the book to Martha and Roddy; they didn't need to meet. And he could have made love to her, got her pregnant. Only his body's apparently inexplicable refusal to perform had prevented it, and yet what a disaster it would have been. He would never use the word 'dickhead' again. It was grossly unfair. His dick was the only part of him that had shown the slightest spark of intelligence.

All this was comforting, in a way. It raised his morale not to have to see himself as Lauren's victim. Determined to start work on the book again, he went into his study, only to stop short in the doorway. For there, propped up on his chair, obviously not forgotten, left deliberately, was Lauren's last painting of the river.

The sun hung over the water, a dull red without rays and without heat, as it might look in the last days of the planet. Beneath was an almost abstract swirl of greys and browns, and in the bottom right-hand corner, barely in the picture, a dark figure, himself, looking out over the water.

EIGHTEEN

All the way through his conversation with Lauren he'd been aware of the answering machine's irritating beep. When he finally played it back, the messages included five requests for telephone interviews about the Kelsey murder. Because of his special interest in conduct disorder he was usually asked for his opinion whenever a crime involving children hit the headlines. Some of these interviews he would have to do, but he didn't feel like calling anybody back at the moment. Lauren's departure was too raw, and he needed to plan how he was going to respond to questions about Danny.

The person he needed to talk to now was Martha. He reached her at the third attempt. She said she'd come round and he went to the window to wait for her. Downstairs, in the kitchen, the answering machine clicked on again. He couldn't make out most of the words, but he thought he heard Danny's name. Leaning over the banister, listening to the voice, he felt a tremor of foreboding, and for the first time understood how hounded Danny must feel.

A gust of wind buffeted the glass, and splashes of rain began to darken the pavement. He watched Martha park the car and run towards the house. She burst in, laughing, running her fingers through her short, dark hair. 'I hope to God it's better than this tomorrow,' she said, as he took her coat.

'Why tomorrow?'

'I'm going to a wedding. In fact I'm the chief bridesmaid. I won't tell you how many times that makes it. But it's a hell of a lot more than three.'

They walked through into the living room. He saw her noticing the gaps, the absences.

'Of course, I wish now I wasn't going. Ian,' she said, when he looked puzzled. 'The murder.'

'You're allowed a private life.'

'Yeah.' She sat down, and laughed. 'I just wish I was better at it.'

He glanced round the half-empty room. 'Yeah, me too.'

The rain was heavier now, pelting against the glass, sealing them in. It was dark in the room, but Tom didn't want the glare of electric light. Martha's face was a pale oval. He sat down opposite her, lowering himself into the chair. That was another thing he'd noticed: he was moving like a much older man, levering himself out of bed in the mornings, leaning on the banisters when he climbed the stairs, as if the injury were physical.

'As you can see,' he said heavily, 'Lauren's moved out.'

'Yes.' She wasted no time on expressions of regret, and he was grateful to her for that. 'And I gather Danny showed up in the middle of it?'

That was the first time she'd used his real name. 'Yes. I could've done without that.'

'He's frightened.'

'Is he exaggerating the risk, do you think?'

In the kitchen the answering machine clicked on again.

'I'm being pursued,' Tom said, listening.

'Well, that's the answer, isn't it?'

'They'd be ringing me anyway. Every time there's a child involved in a serious crime . . .' He waved in the direction of the voice.

'Like this?'

'No, this is a bit worse. I'm not returning the calls. But no, you're right. Something happened when Danny came to the house. A lot of things had gone, so it looked empty, and I don't know whether you've noticed, but it sounds different as well, hollow, and Danny was in the middle of all this, and I suddenly thought, I shouldn't be doing this. I mean – what I'm trying to say is, You don't want an empty space at the centre of your life when you've got somebody like Danny prowling round the edges. He's always pressing for more, you know? And the emptiness gives him a way in.'

'You make him sound like a virus.'

Tom shrugged. 'He's dangerous.'

'Violent?'

'Don't know. Probably not.'

'Probably not?'

'Yeah. Probably. I don't know, you don't know, the parole board certainly didn't know. I suspect Danny doesn't know.'

She was listening intently. It was curious this feeling of intimacy, in the darkening room. 'Are you sure that's a fair assessment?' she asked. 'I'm wondering a bit whether you don't see him as threatening because you're . . . feeling threatened anyway. I know what it's like when a relationship breaks up – my God, I ought to. You *do* feel threatened.'

'You mean, I'm cracking up?'

'Of course I don't mean that.'

'Oh, I don't know, you might. Might be true. Did you know he accused a teacher at Long Garth of sexual abuse?'

She looked surprised. 'Are you sure? There's nothing on the file.'

'The headmaster decided a public investigation wouldn't be in anybody's best interests.'

'So the teacher got away with it.'

'Or Danny.'

'You think he was lying?'

'I don't know. The teacher had been bending the rules, but then people always do bend the rules with Danny.'

Martha was worried. 'Do you want to give up?'

'No, in fact I'm seeing him again tonight. I suppose I'm just reminding myself to be careful.'

'How's it going?'

'Too soon to say. Danny's agenda gets clearer all the time. Everything I said about him at the trial's been systematically contradicted.'

'Convincingly?'

Tom hesitated. 'Persuasively. But he hasn't got on to the murder yet, and that's when reality'll start to bite. And of course at the moment he's distracted by this other case.'

'Well, it must be a hell of a shock to open a paper and find your own photograph there. After all these years.'

'I suggested giving it a rest for a while, but he says he wants to press on.'

'He needs to do it. And there mightn't be that much time. They'll be looking for him.'

'Could they find him?'

'They can find anybody. If they want to badly enough. And this is a very good story. Here are these two little thugs – and what do you know? Here's this other little thug they've just let out. Are we too soft on crime? Should life mean life? It's gold dust.'

'It's depressing.'

'Yeah, well . . . I wish I wasn't going.'

'To the wedding?'

'Yes. Though it's not that far. It's only York.' She sat brooding. 'If it gets too bad we'll have to move him.'

'I don't see the point of a false identity if it can be broken as easily as this.'

'It's just bad luck. He could've gone ten years before anything like this happened.'

Tom thought for a moment. 'Okay. Suppose it blows up while you're away?'

'He's got my mobile number. Obviously, I can't leave it switched on all the time, but I'll keep checking. And he's got two emergency numbers he can ring, but that's only if things go really pear-shaped. Anyway, he knows when to use them. There shouldn't be a problem, and even if there is, there's no need for you to be involved.'

'Well, good.' He looked round. 'I'm trying to think if there's anything else.'

'We've got it covered, Tom. There's no need to worry.'

'All right.'

She looked at her watch. 'And I'd better get me skates on. I promised I'd be there in time for a final fitting.'

'Are you driving?'

'Of course. I might need to get back early.'

They said goodbye on the doorstep. Martha turned up her collar against the wind and rain.

'Get your priorities right, Martha.'

'I know, I know. Enjoy myself.'

'No. Catch the bloody bouquet!'

'Oh, you still advocate marriage, do you?'

He smiled. 'Ye-es.'

She reached up and kissed his cheek. 'Bye, Tom. See you when I get back.'

NINETEEN

The phone rang at intervals throughout the afternoon. After calling his mother and his secretary to explain the situation, Tom left the answering machine on, and closed the kitchen door so he didn't have to hear the messages. He spent three hours rearranging the furniture to make the living room look less bare. He brought a table and two chairs down from the spare bedroom, and some paintings down from the loft. Then he decided it was cold enough, certainly wet enough, to justify lighting a fire. The coal was damp, and spat and smoked miserably, but he persevered and managed to coax it into flame. When it was going to his satisfaction, he poured himself a drink. Probably he should have made himself something to eat, but that meant the kitchen, and the kitchen meant the answering machine, so he decided not to bother.

With the fire lit and the lamps on, the living room looked less desolate than he would have believed possible a few hours ago. It still sounded hollow, and the way the furniture clustered round the hearth was a little too reminiscent of a campfire, but he was aware, as he looked around him, of a shiver of excitement, barely distinguishable from fear. He was free. Perhaps he ought to go away for a few days, sort out what he felt, but he was conscious of a countervailing desire to go to ground, to pull the tattered remnants of his life around him. Keep out the cold. And meanwhile, only an hour or so away, there was Danny, whose problems dwarfed his own.

He switched on the news. The Kelsey murder was the second item. Close-ups of flowers left at the scene of the crime, blowzy chrysanthemums, 'Love' in blue ink dribbling down a wet card. Then pictures of a white van accelerating rapidly, pursued by angry crowds.

The doorbell rang. Danny. Tom walked through his hollow house, his footsteps, even his breathing, sounding different inside the changed space, and let him in.

'Did you get Martha?' Danny asked.

'Yes, she came round.'

'Do you know she's going away tonight?'

'Yes.'

'I don't know why she can't cancel.'

'It's a wedding. She's the bridesmaid.'

'She ought to've seen this coming.'

'I don't see how she could have done. The boys were only charged yesterday. Anyway, come through.'

'Did you see the news?' Danny asked, following him into the consulting room.

'Yes. They didn't mention you this time.'

'They're on to me, though. I'm sure I was followed.'

He found it difficult to settle, rubbing the backs of his hands, wriggling in the chair. There was no way of knowing whether his conviction that he was being followed was paranoid or not. It could be true.

'By the way,' Tom said, settling down into his chair, 'I went to see Angus MacDonald.'

Danny said nothing at all, just stared at him blankly.

'He asked me to give you his address.'

Tom scribbled Scarsdale Writers' Centre and the address on the back of an envelope, and handed it to Danny, who took it, looked at it and put it in his pocket, all without saying anything. He seemed too dazed to take it in.

'Look,' Tom said, 'shall we take things a bit easy this time?'

Danny was already shaking his head. 'No, now or never.'

He was reaching for his cigarettes as he spoke. Tom sensed a new tension in him, a new purpose. Familiar sounds – the creak of a chair, the popping of the gas fire; familiar smells – furniture polish, wet wool, the smoke on Danny's clothes and hair; familiar sights – the circle of reddish light on the desk, Danny's left forefinger picking at a torn cuticle.

'Lizzie,' Danny said.

'Don't rush.'

Tom sat back, waited, let the silence re-create the space around them. Danny was tapping his cigarette, planning, Tom thought, the shortest route. The atmosphere was different tonight. Partly because Danny was desperate, trying to dismiss the threat of newspaper intrusion from his mind, but partly too because Tom's recent conversation with Angus had alerted him to the possibility that Danny might be lying. *Might* be. Tom wasn't sure, now, which of them he believed. Angus had his own reasons to lie.

Curiously, as if reading his thoughts, Danny began talking about Angus. 'When I was at Long Garth I invented a twin. I told everybody I was a twin, and that the other one had died. I think it was . . . well, it's obvious what it was, but nobody said, "No, you're not. You never had a twin." Because the past didn't matter. Angus was the only person who said: "No, sorry, Danny. No twin. Just you."' He laughed. 'And that was actually quite a sharp jerk on the leash. Suddenly there was this objective truth, and I couldn't get round it. He wouldn't let me.'

'Did you ever talk to Angus about Lizzie? I don't mean the murder . . .'

'Wrote. Not talked.'

'Do you think you could try now?'

A deep drag on the cigarette, flared nostrils, he looked like an athlete contemplating a jump he probably wouldn't make.

'She was an old lady,' he said at last, with a sigh. 'I know it sounds odd when I call her Lizzie, like, you know, sort of disrespectful, but we all called her that. She was a local character, always the same coat, the same shopping bag. She had these very thick lenses in her glasses, because she'd had cataracts. My mother always used to stop and talk to her, and one of the things you noticed was that she couldn't have a conversation without her lips moving while the other person spoke. You know, as if she was trying to speak for them. Somebody must have made her self-conscious about it, because she had a habit of putting a hand up to her mouth and trying to hold her lips still. Very thin, pleated upper lip. False teeth, too even, but yellow, age spots on her hands, a wedding ring, swollen knuckles. I remember looking at the ring and wondering how she got it off her finger. It was marooned, you know, very loose, but stranded by the swollen knuckle.'

Tom was remembering a photograph of Lizzie's left hand, a close-up of the injuries inflicted when the murderer had tried to wrench the ring off.

'She had huge pupils, they didn't change in size, they didn't respond to the light, and she used to bend down and ask me questions about school, and her breath smelt of peppermints. Oh, and the bag smelt of fish. It was an old canvas shopping bag, and it used to swing from side to side and hit her on the leg.'

'How old did you think she was?'

'She was seventy-eight.'

'No. How old did you *think* she was?'

'Oh ancient. Ancient.'

'What sort of person was she?'

'Lonely old lady, widow, lived by herself, kept cats, befriended strays, there was always room for another. She was very protective of the cats. Once Paul and me – a kid I used to go to school with – were playing with one of the kittens, and she came running out to chase us away. She just assumed we were teasing it.'

'And were you?'

'No.' A pause. 'I suppose the short answer is, I don't know what sort of person she was. Because "lonely old lady, kept cats" is just a stereotype, isn't it? She could've been anything.'

'Can we turn now to the day it happened? Do you remember how you were feeling that day?'

'Weird. It was the day after the vicar came round, and Mum had her great attempt at beating me with Dad's belt. I ran out of the house. I ran miles.'

'And next morning?'

'I lay in bed. She didn't say: "Are you getting up?" or anything like that. I knew everything had changed. I'd kicked away the ground under my feet. I got up, she wasn't in, and I just wandered off. I seemed to be floating and when I came round I was in the lane by Lizzie's house, and she was coming out, going to the shops. She had this old shopping bag with her. I watched her. I don't know why I watched her, I just did. She got to the corner of the street, and then she turned round and came back, shook the door handle and then set off again. I suppose her memory must have been starting to fail a bit. She came right past me, and instead of saying "Hello", I stepped back into the alley and she didn't see me.'

'Did you know what you were going to do?'

'Yes. I knew where the key was. All this going back to check the door was locked, and then she left a spare key under a plant-pot in the backyard. As soon as she'd turned the corner, I walked up the alley, got the key and went in.'

A long pause, but the time for prompting was past.

'I'd been in the house before. Once when she went to hospital for a few days for her cataract operation my mother said she'd feed the cats, so we used to walk down together and do that. I went into the living room and looked round. There weren't any cats in sight. Then I saw one ginger one at the top of the stairs, but it ran away when it saw me. There were all kinds of rumours about how much money she had, she was supposed to have masses stacked away. When I went with my mother she looked in the fridge, and there were all these cod steaks, but my mother said they weren't for her, they were for the cats. I think she spent all her pension money on the cats. She used to have a handful of dry cornflakes for her breakfast, that was all. You'd see her on the front doorstep when you were walking to school, eating these dry cornflakes, and my mother used to say, "That's all she ever has. She's not feeding herself." ' He paused. 'She was a tiny little woman. Just skin and bones.'

Danny seemed to be losing his way. At the same time, Tom thought this detailed re-creation of Lizzie had its own value. He waited, but there was nothing else. 'So there you are in the house,' Tom said. 'What happened next?'

'I started looking for money. I found some loose change on the mantelpiece, couple of quid for the insurance man, and then I went upstairs and started looking round her bedroom. There was a musty smell, and some sort of peach-coloured powder on the dressing-table top. I rubbed it between my fingers, and . . .' He seemed surprised by the banality, the emptiness of his own recollections. 'I just stood, looking in the mirror, and the face didn't look like mine.'

Under his normal voice, a child's piping treble was faintly audible, growing clearer by the minute. Danny was producing this sound without sign of strain, without a hint of falsetto, and seemed to be unaware that he was doing it. Tom felt a prickling at the back of his neck.

'I don't know why she came back, because she'd already checked that she'd locked the door. Perhaps she was checking she'd turned the gas off. Anyway, I heard the key turn in the lock, and she's coming in. I look round for somewhere to hide . . .' His eyes were closing. 'The bed's a divan, I can't get underneath, I have to get in the wardrobe. I push the clothes along, and I get right in the back and close the door. It's pitch black, everything stinks of mothballs, and fur. My face is pressed into fur, and there's something on my cheek. It's a fox's nose, a real fox with glass eyes, and its paws are dangling.'

Danny's hair was damp with sweat. Tom said, 'It's not happening now, Danny.'

His eyes opened, the pupils huge, glutted on darkness. 'No, I know. I pushed it away from me, and the wardrobe banged against the wall. I'm like, don't come up, don't come up, but she must have heard the bang. The living-room door opens – opened – and I know she's standing at the foot of the stairs, listening. I go very quiet. I can't breathe, the fur's up my nose, and, you know, I . . . I can't, I can't, I've got to breathe, so I push my way out, and she's coming up the stairs. So I run – ran – on to the landing, she didn't hear, she didn't look up. There's a parting in her hair, a line of pink, and I know there's only seconds before she looks up and sees me. I've got to get out. So I run down the first four stairs to the half landing . . . And she's seen me. She won't back off, she says: "What you doing, you little bugger?" I've got to get past, so I put my hands on the banisters and kick her in the chest, and she falls backwards. Slowly, ever so slowly, but she can't have done, can she? It can't have been slow.'

He was staring at Tom, as if the answer to this question might change everything.

'And then the next thing is she's lying at the foot of the stairs. Her face has gone all red because her legs are halfway up the stairs, and all the blood's drained down into her head. Her eyes are closed, just little slits of white, and I – I don't know what I thought. I'd got beyond thinking. I –'

'Danny,' Tom said again. 'It's not happening now.'

Danny widened his eyes with the look of somebody waking from a long sleep, and blinked several times.

'Do you want to stop?' Tom asked.

A deep sigh. When he spoke again his voice was deeper, but then shaded up again into a treble. 'No. I'm looking down at her. One of her shoes has come off and it's lying next to her face. She doesn't move, I can see right up her nostrils, and I'm like trying to get past without touching her.'

'She's unconscious?'

'Yes, I suppose so.' He sounded dazed. 'I thought she might grab hold of me as I went past, but she didn't.'

'What happened next?'

'I'm kneeling beside her, I put the cushion –'

'Where did the cushion come from?'

A blank stare. 'From the living room. It must have done, mustn't it? I must've gone into the living room and got it. I put the cushion over her face, and pressed . . .'

'Do you know why you did that?'

He'd gone very white. 'I don't want to see her eyes. I don't want her looking at me.'

'You could go away.'

No answer.

'Are you frightened because you know she'll tell your mother?'

Danny's thumb moved up to his mouth and, under the pretext of biting his nail, he sucked. 'I suppose so.'

'What were you feeling when you did that? Can you remember?'

'Just peaceful. Deep water, no buzzing. Quiet.'

'Was there ever a time when you thought you should stop?'

'No.'

'And you weren't frightened? Or angry?'

'No. I was later, frightened, but not then. I lifted the cushion off and she'd been sick. I think I remember her thrashing about, because I thought she was trying to get away, and I pressed down harder, but it can't have been that, can it? She must've been . . .'

Tom waited and waited until, at last, the word popped out of Danny's mouth, as improbable as a toad.

'. . . dying.'

'And what did you feel then?'

'Nothing. Just tired.'

'When did you start . . . when did you realize what you'd done?'

'I don't know. I'm not sure I did. I was dazed.'

238

'Frightened?'

'I suppose so, I don't know. I don't know whether I'm thinking I must've been frightened, so . . . I don't know. I'm scared shitless now.'

He reeked of sweat. Tom was beginning to wonder how much further this could be allowed to continue. He had to balance Danny's desire to press on with the knowledge that worse was to come. 'What did you do next?'

'Went into town and played *Space Invaders*.'

'With the insurance money?'

'Yes.'

'Do you see how that seemed to other people?'

'Yeah. Rotten psychopathic little bastard, didn't give a shit. Let's hammer him.' Danny shook his head. 'Wasn't how it felt.'

'How did you feel?'

'Like a chicken with its head off.'

'And then you went back home?'

'Yeah, had my tea, threw up, which was good actually because my mother decided I was ill, so I went to bed early and hid under the clothes. I kept getting flashes, you know, Lizzie's face, and I heard her coming up the stairs again, but this time they were our stairs. And she sort of leapt across the room, right into my face. And I wet the bed. I kept jabbing myself with a sharp pencil to keep myself awake because I didn't dare go to sleep. And in the morning when I got up I somehow thought that everybody knew, I thought it would've leaked out somehow, but it was just normal. Nobody knew.'

'And then you went back,' Tom said flatly, surprised himself by the brutality of his return to the facts.

'Yes,' Danny said, on an exhaled breath.

'Why? When you were so frightened you were jabbing pencils into yourself to stay awake?'

'I wanted to see if she was still dead.'

A pause. Tom considered the various options open to him. The truth, he thought. 'No, Danny, I can't accept that. You knew she was dead.'

'I was ten years old.'

No breathless treble now, but a hard, grinding, angry adult voice.

'Yes,' Tom said steadily. 'And I think it's quite true – a lot of ten-year-olds don't understand death. They don't realize it's permanent. But I think you did.'

'You just don't want to admit you got it wrong.'

'What did I get wrong?'

'Telling the court I knew what I'd done. Have you ever stood outside a junior school and watched the kids come out? The biggest kids, the "big boys"? They're *tiny*. I was like that.'

'I know. I remember. I still say you knew death was permanent.'

A braying laugh. 'Because of the fucking chicken?'

'Because you lived on a farm. Because you witnessed the deaths of animals, because you took part in killing them, because your grandfather had died, and

240

you knew bloody well he hadn't come back, because you were frightened when your mother went into hospital for the second mastectomy. You thought she was going to die, and you knew bloody well that didn't mean she was going to be away till teatime. You were frightened you were going to lose her. You were frightened she'd never come back.'

Danny said deliberately, 'When I went back to Lizzie's, part of me thought she wouldn't still be there.'

Tom nodded. 'Go on.'

'She was just lying there. She'd changed, her skin was a different colour, darker, and the cats were yowling all over the place.'

'So what did you do?'

'I fed the cats.'

Up till this moment Tom had been able to suspend his knowledge of the forensic evidence, to listen to Danny's story as if this were his only source of information. Now, suddenly, there was a chorus of muffled voices in the background. Thirteen years ago, everybody had told Tom about the feeding of the cats, in a tone of voice that suggested it merely amplified the horror. 'And then he fed the cats.'

'Why?'

'They were starving.'

Domestic animals were inside Danny's moral circle, Tom thought, as they had been inside his father's. 'So you fed the cats? Then what?'

'Nothing.'

'Do you remember what happened?'

'Nothing happened. I fed the cats and I went home.'

'You were there for five hours. You were seen going in and you were seen coming out.'

Those five hours, for the police who'd investigated the case, for everybody who'd been involved in any way, were the heart of the darkness, the source of that look of frozen disgust that Tom remembered so vividly from the trial. Nigel Lewis, showing Tom photographs of scuff marks on the carpet where Lizzie had been dragged across the floor, had said: 'He played with her.' The horror in his voice could still raise hairs on the nape of Tom's neck thirteen years later.

'You moved her, Danny.'

'I never touched her.'

'You did. Look, if you don't want to do this, that's fine. Perhaps there's things you shouldn't say, perhaps there's things you can't say. But there's no point lying. There's no point coming this far and then telling lies. It's a waste of what you've put yourself through to get here.'

A long silence. No sound but their breathing, which suddenly seemed loud.

'There's nothing there,' Danny said. 'People say five hours. Okay, I have to believe it, but what I remember covers about ten minutes. I looked at her, I fed the cats, I made sure the doors were open, so the mother cat could get in and out, I went home. I know what the police thought, they thought I molested her. Even though there was no evidence, even though I was only ten, they still thought that.' He leant forward. 'But you know, I wasn't sexually abused. I didn't have that kind of awareness. I didn't have a sex drive, for God's sake. Plus she was seventy-eight.'

'And dead.'

'And dead.'

'What did she look like? Try to imagine you're looking down at her. What are you thinking?'

'She's like a doll. She can't do anything. She can't hurt me, or shout, or anything. It's stupid to be frightened. All that stuff about her coming upstairs –'

'Your stairs?'

'Yes – it's rubbish. She can't even move.'

Silence. Danny seemed to be dragging himself back from a great distance. 'You talk about me putting myself through this for no reason. Well, it is for no reason. I don't know why I killed her. I didn't know then, and I don't know now. And I don't know how to live with it.'

They broke there. Danny's speech was slurred. Tom made him a cup of coffee, then spent twenty minutes trying to calm him down. Danny was dreading the journey home. On the doorstep, turning to look back, he said, 'I know you don't believe me, but I am being followed.'

Tom was aware, almost telepathically, of every stage of Danny's journey home: rocking backwards and forwards on the Metro, gazing blank-eyed at the advertisements opposite, while grey walls lined with bunched and corded cables hurtle past. Then the train glides to a halt between graffiti-daubed walls. Danny gets out and pushes his ticket into the turnstile, which disgorges him into a night of rain and wind, of orange light smeared over greasy streets, and then, turning up his coat against the cold, he's away from the lights and crowds, striding down dark streets, where once-imposing houses loom over him, until he goes down a flight of steps to a basement flat, takes out a key, lets himself in. And there, in the dingy hall with its black-and-white tiles and single naked bulb, Tom loses him.

TWENTY

Tom did one press interview in connection with the Kelsey murder. As the journalist was getting ready to go, she asked casually about Tom's connection with Danny Miller, and, looking down into her open bag, Tom saw the red light on her tape recorder still lit. He smiled, and denied all knowledge of Danny's current whereabouts.

He spent Friday night and most of Saturday with his mother. She was saddened by the breakdown of his marriage, but not surprised. She didn't say: 'I told you so.' She didn't discover that she'd always disliked and distrusted Lauren. In fact she did everything right, but still he was glad to get away.

Back home, he found himself with that curious suspended feeling that comes from having spent the night in your childhood home, a sense that adult life had been put on hold. Everything about it was unsettling. The single bed, so narrow he'd woken in the middle of the night with his arm flung out into empty space, the wonky headboard, the curtain and carpet patterns that seemed mysteriously to have soaked up the sweats and nightmares of his childhood fevers and breathed them out again into the air as he tossed and turned and tried to sleep.

In spite of his bad night, he was restless now, full of energy. Just as well, perhaps, since he'd agreed to take part in a television discussion later that night. His first reaction had been to say no, but contributing to the public debate on how young offenders should be treated was, after all, part of his job.

He played back the answering machine, took notes on the calls, then slumped in front of the television for an hour. He'd have liked to have gone for a jog to calm himself down, but the weather, which had been close and sticky all day, seemed about to break. He saw through the bay window the massing of black clouds, sagging over the rooftops like a tarpaulin full of water, though for the moment there was no rain, only this hot, brooding intensity. Then a flash of lightning, and the first spattering of raindrops on the glass.

He was about to pour himself a drink when the phone rang.

'It's Danny,' a whispering voice said.

Tom opened his mouth to reply, but something wrong in the voice stopped him. He stayed silent, aware of his breathing, knowing it must be audible at the other end. Heavy breathing call in reverse, he thought. Bloody ridiculous. A minute, two minutes, then the receiver was softly replaced.

Somebody checking, obviously. Thank God he'd had the sense to keep quiet. He drew the curtains, lit a fire, piled logs on to it, thinking a good blaze would be pleasant to come home to. The worst times for missing Lauren were coming back to an empty house, though he'd been doing it for over a year, he should be used to it by now. But a fire helped.

He was watching the second half of a thriller, and he'd long since lost track of the plot, but the fire blazed away, his face felt swollen and numb with heat, and still the wind moaned around the house. Somewhere a gate was banging. Probably the postgrad students next door had left their gate off the latch. He got up to look. Pulling the curtain back, he saw what at first he took to be his own face reflected in the glass, until a sudden movement dislocated the illusion. Pale features, lank wet hair, distorted by streaming rivulets of rain.

They stared at each other, and then the intruder turned and ran down the gleaming road. By the time Tom got to the door he'd disappeared. Probably he should phone the police, but there wasn't time. He had to leave for the television studios in twenty minutes. Better check the back-garden door was bolted, and make sure all the doors and windows were locked. Could be a peeping tom or somebody looking for an empty house to burgle. No real reason to suppose it was connected with Danny.

Before leaving the house he made sure the burglar alarm was primed, and then stood looking up and down the street, which was as empty as it always was at this time of night.

Tom never liked studio discussions. Sweating under the hot lights, remembering to sit on the hem of his jacket, resigned to cameras that in the interests of cutting-edge journalism zoomed in on nostrils and ears, and all for the sake of a debate that rapidly got bogged down in the evil effects of point-and-shoot video games. One of the twelve-year-olds charged with Mrs Kelsey's murder had been addicted to such games, or so the newspapers claimed – along with a few thousand other kids who'd never killed anybody. Afterwards they adjourned to the Green Room, where a far more interesting and honest discussion took place over glasses of warm white wine. Tom was offered help in getting his make-up off, but since he was driving straight home decided not to bother. He left the studio feeling that nothing new had been contributed – not in front of the cameras anyway – and that he was as much to blame for this as anyone.

How desperate people were for an explanation – any explanation, as long as it was simple – and how difficult it was to supply one. No, not difficult, imposs-ible. He was remembering that once he and Lauren had become involved in a local opera group's pro-duction of Britten's *The Turn of the Screw*. Lauren had been asked to design the sets, a task that suited her particular talents very well. Huge, light-filled backdrops of sky and estuary, the tower, the lake, the copse with its bare branches and black nests like clots of blood in veins. He'd been dragged in as a production assistant, and in rehearsal must have heard every note of the score, every word of the libretto, a dozen times or more, though all he remembered now was Miles's song, his little Latin mnemonic.

> Malo: I would rather be
> Malo: in an apple tree
> Malo: than a naughty boy
> Malo: in adversity

No animals in the opera, for obvious reasons. No animals in the novella either, though children living on a country estate would have been surrounded by them. But animals give the game away. Are the children really evil? Or is the governess mad? Any halfway-decent vet could've sorted that out in seconds. Disturbed children torture animals.

Danny didn't. That had struck Tom from the beginning. All those neglected, used, abused, dead or dying animals, but Danny had not been cruel to any of them. Or so Danny said. But then Danny's story, though Tom believed him to be telling the truth, most of the time, was not all it appeared to be. His apparently rambling excursions into the past were anything but rambling. He was constructing a systematic rebuttal of the evidence Tom had given in court. There was a good deal of antagonism in all this. More than Tom had realized at the start.

It took him ten minutes to get home, and another five before he found a parking space in a side street several hundred yards from his front door. The street was deserted, the lamps a line of orange flowers blossoming in puddles. He walked quickly back to the main road, his footsteps echoing amongst the empty warehouses that rose, tall and black, into the night sky, ghost smells of the goods they'd once contained – sharp, sweet, sour – fading on the air. He turned the corner, and noticed a solitary figure outside his house, advancing a little way down the road, then going back up the steps into the shadow of the porch.

Tom quickened his pace. 'Danny,' he said, when he was close enough to be heard without raising his voice. 'What on earth are you doing here?'

'Somebody's following me.'

He looked deranged, slack mouthed and sweating, but there was no doubting the reality of the fear. Tom could smell it on him. 'You'd better come in,' he said, unlocking the front door and stepping quickly inside to switch off the burglar alarm. He walked ahead of Danny into the living room, not bothering to switch on the hall lights.

'Can you pull the curtains to?' Danny asked, lingering in the doorway.

Tom made sure the folds of material overlapped at the centre so that no chink of light could show through, and then he turned to the drinks table. Normally he never offered clients alcohol, but this wasn't a proper session, and he needed a drink himself. He felt high after the TV interview, vapidly talkative, mentally flatulent, deeply distrustful of himself. Talking to the media produces exactly the same kind of unfocused anxiety as a night of heavy drinking. He raised a hand to his face, and his fingers slipped on skin greasy with make-up and sweat, as if he were wearing a rapidly disintegrating mask. And now, to all this, was added the strangeness of having Danny here, in his half-empty, booming living room, agitated, scared, in what felt like the middle of the night. But wasn't, he reminded himself with a glance at his watch. It was still twenty minutes short of midnight.

'Whisky?' he asked.

Danny sat down, slumped rather, in one of the armchairs. He looked up and said: 'Yes. Please.'

Tom handed him a full glass, and settled on the other side of the fireplace. The fire had burnt low, and he spent a few minutes feeding nuggets of coal into the glowing caverns. A domestic scene, he thought, looking round the walls that seemed less bare, now, than they had by day, the squares left by Lauren's pictures obscured by leaping shadows.

'Well now, what's been happening?'

'I was followed.' Danny's voice had the strident

pitch of somebody who doesn't expect to be believed. 'I was working in the library, and there was a man at the end of the street when I left, and I noticed in Grey Street he was still there, and then he got on the same train as me. He sat at the other end of the carriage.'

'Did you recognize him?'

'No.'

'Isn't it possible he was just going the same way?'

A quick, stubborn shake of the head.

'Did he get off at the same stop?'

'I didn't wait to find out. I got off the stop before, you know, waited till the last possible second then made a dash for the door, and then I ran across the bridge, down the other side, and jumped on a train coming back into town.'

'Do you think you lost him?'

'I don't know.'

'Who do you think it was?'

'A reporter. Or somebody who wants to beat the shit out of me, I don't know. I daren't go back to the flat.'

'I'll phone Martha,' Tom said.

Martha was on her answering machine. He left a message, remembered the wedding, tried her mobile, left another message. 'Is there anybody else we can phone?'

'Not really.'

'Martha said you had numbers you could phone.'

'Yeah, but they're in the flat.'

So much for Martha's claim to have everything covered. 'What about the police?'

'No, not yet. They don't know. Only the chief constable knows. And what am I going to tell them? Somebody followed me? No, it's best if we wait for Martha. She's probably at the reception.'

Tom poured himself and Danny another generous whisky, and threw a log on the fire. There was quite a good blaze going now. 'It's a pity we didn't record our sessions,' he said. 'You could've burnt the tapes.'

'It's a gimmick. You know as well as I do things can't be left behind like that. And anyway, I'd have to burn you too.'

'Can I ask you something?' Tom said. 'Was it a coincidence, you jumping in the river like that?'

'A hundred yards away from your house? No, of course it wasn't. I'd been following you for days.'

'Why?'

A shrug. 'Wanted to talk. And every time I didn't ring the doorbell, I got more and more depressed, and angry, not with you, with myself. It wasn't . . .' He tried again. 'It wasn't a great plot. I didn't think, Oh, if I jump in the river and he comes in after me, we'll both be drowned and serve him bloody right. I wasn't thinking like that. I wasn't thinking at all. I just wanted the pain to stop.'

Tom was becoming puzzled by Danny's movements, which seemed to be a curious mixture of agitation and paralysis. He was – not twitching, the movements weren't as rapid as that – but shifting his gaze about the room, glancing over his shoulder, looking from side to side. His glances, his gestures, were considerably more disturbed than his speech.

'What're you looking at, Danny?'

'Nothing.'

No eye contact, and then, unnervingly, his eyes focused on something behind, and a little to the right, of Tom's head.

'Do you ever see her?' he asked gently.

'No, I'm not quick enough.'

'You mean, she's been there, but –'

'I'm always just missing her.'

'Does she ever say anything?'

'No.'

'So how do you know she's there?'

'Because she leaves things.'

'Like what?'

'Hair. There's always a ball of hair in the bathroom.'

Tom was thinking that almost certainly this present mood was the closest he would ever get to understanding Danny's state of mind in the missing five hours he'd spent alone with Lizzie's corpse. 'What did you do to her, Danny?'

His speech was slurred. 'Made her do things.'

'What sort of things?'

'Things.'

Again, Tom saw the photographs: the marks on

Lizzie's ankles, wrists and upper chest, inflicted – so the pathologist had said – after death.

He played with her.

No point pressing for more now or, perhaps, ever. Pressing him now might well force him over the edge.

Silence. Danny's eyelids looked swollen, he seemed to be drifting off to sleep, but then he said, 'Do you believe in evil?'

A perfectly sane question. A lot easier to deal with than balls of hair in the bathroom. Tom, his mind full of alternative ways of getting hold of Martha – would Mike Freeman be likely to know where she was staying? – answered, almost absently: 'In the meta-physical sense? No, I don't. But as a word to describe certain kinds of behaviour, I've no problems with it. It's just the word we've agreed to use to describe certain kinds of action. And I don't think it's an alternative to other ways of describing the same things. There's no logical reason why "mad" and "bad" should be alternatives.'

'And people? Do you think people can be evil?'

'I suppose if somebody's entire life is dedicated to performing evil actions, yes. But if you mean yourself . . . Killing Lizzie was an evil thing to do, but I don't think *you* were evil when you did it, and I certainly don't think you are now.'

'There's something I've never told anybody. Well, actually, I did tell you, but I don't think you picked up on it. You know when I hid in the wardrobe? It was pitch black in there, there wasn't a chink of light anywhere.' He was whispering. 'But I saw the fox.'

Tom said carefully, 'Memory plays all sorts of tricks, Danny. You knew what was in there. You saw it when you opened the door, and then you felt it, you felt it in the dark and you've remembered touch as sight.'

'Yeah, I suppose so.'

He didn't sound convinced, and Tom was glad when he could turn away and resume his search for numbers. He'd found Mike Freeman's number, but it was well past midnight now, and what explanation could he give for calling him? Perhaps it would be more sensible to make up a bed for Danny on the sofa, and try to sort things out in the morning.

He put down the phone book. 'Look, I think it might be better if we tried to get some sleep. Martha's obviously not going to ring now, and you need to get some rest.'

'I won't sleep.'

'Well, at least lie down. I'll get some pillows.'

Upstairs in the bathroom, in the act of pulling clean pillow slips out of the airing cupboard, Tom caught sight of himself in the mirror, and was shocked. Sweat, dissolving make-up, bags under his eyes: not a pretty sight. A shower, that's what he needed, and then bed. Please, God, bed. The adrenalin rush of the TV debate had drained away, and, trailing pillows and sheets downstairs, he felt positively doddery.

Danny hadn't moved. 'Would you like some sleeping pills?' Tom asked.

'No, I'd better not. I'm trying to get off them.'

Tom made up a rough bed on the sofa, and went to fetch a glass of water from the kitchen.

When he returned, Danny had switched off the lamp and was lying under a sheet in the firelight. An arm and one side of his face and neck were etched in trembling gold. Poor bloody Angus, Tom thought, looking down at him, you didn't stand a chance.

'Goodnight,' he said, as he prepared to close the door. 'Don't worry, there's a phone in my room, so I'll hear it all right if Martha calls.'

TWENTY-ONE

Tom lay in the dark, too tired to think, too tired not to. He had all the physical symptoms of fear, and this surprised him, because there was nothing of which he needed to be afraid. He was worried about Danny's state of mind, but that was a different matter. No point thinking about it now. Resolutely, he turned on his side, and soon after dropped over the edge into sleep.

His dream-self was not so biddable. He was on a demolition site standing by a fire, and a man whom he did not recognize was walking towards him from the other side of the fire, a dark shape shimmering in the heat. The man, still faceless, came closer and began throwing tapes on to the fire. Not cassettes, but the tape itself, masses of it, brown, shiny coils that lay on the hot timbers, not shrivelling in a single spurt of flame – as, even in the dream, Tom knew that they should – but writhing, in what looked like prolonged agony.

He woke, sweating, wiping the back of his hand across his neck, convinced he could smell burning, though a second later he identified this as an illusion left over from the dream. Then, as he was turning over to try to get back to sleep, he heard Danny moving about downstairs, dragging something heavy across the floor.

In the context of their last session it was the most horrible sound he could have heard – *he played with her*.

Grabbing his dressing gown, Tom went out on to the landing. The hall carpet glowed orange in the flickering light from under the living-room door. There shouldn't have been as much light as that. He ran downstairs and had just enough presence of mind to put a hand on the door to check that it was not hot, before he burst into the room.

The fire burnt furiously, piled high with logs. Danny had dragged the log basket on to the hearth rug and was kneeling beside it, a log in each hand, watching the fire burn. Tom went across to him, and saw what until now had been hidden by the basket. A log had toppled out of the grate and fallen on to the hearth rug. Quickly, without thinking, Tom stooped, picked it up and threw it back on to the fire. A second later he was bent double over his burnt hand, stamping on the singed rug with his slippered feet. It hadn't caught fire, and wouldn't now. To make doubly sure, he fetched the jug he'd brought up with the whisky and poured water over the blackened patch. There was a nasty smell of singed wool. He tried to straighten up, but the pain forced him down again. It was almost as if he'd been winded rather than burnt. 'What the fuck are you playing at?' he said.

Danny raised his sleepwalker's eyes. 'I must've nodded off to sleep.'

Kneeling on the floor, Tom wanted to say, with two more logs in your hands? But he didn't say it.

They stared at each other without speaking. Then: 'It's terribly hot in here,' Tom said, keeping his voice casual. 'I don't think we need any more logs on the fire.'

He prised Danny's fingers loose and put the logs back into the basket. Then he said, 'Shall we pull the chairs further back?' Keep the speech slow and soft. Don't crowd him. He was giving Danny lots of room. But the chairs had to be moved. The room was full of the smell of scorched material – a different smell from the singed wool of the rug – and these were old chairs. Whatever stuffing had been used to fill the cushions, it wouldn't be fire-retardant.

At last, with sofa and chairs restored to their original positions, the room looked less like a bonfire waiting to be lit. Danny sat at one end of the sofa, hands clasped between his knees, still staring at the fire. He hadn't spoken or made any move to help Tom with the furniture. He seemed hardly to be aware of his presence.

Tom opened the window and, still half turned towards Danny, leant out, gulping in cold air. Somewhere out there, invisible, though only a few hundred yards from this hot box with its leaping flames, the river flowed, past rotted jetties and crumbling steps, out towards the sea.

The room was cooler now. Sitting in the armchair, Tom began to talk, slowly and calmly. The words didn't matter. At first nothing that he said went in, but then gradually the dazed, swollen look faded from Danny's face. Once he cleared his throat and seemed about to speak, but no words came out.

'Why don't you lie down?' Tom said at last. 'Even if you can't sleep, it might help to rest.'

Danny seemed to understand and stretched out on the sofa. Tom would have liked to dampen down the fire, pile ashes on to the blazing logs, but he didn't dare risk doing that yet. Danny's eyes were still fixed unwaveringly on the flames.

Tom had just brought the footstool closer to his chair, when the front doorbell rang. Who on earth —? It was two o'clock in the morning. Of course it could only be one person. 'Martha!' he said, not bothering to disguise his relief, and ran to let her in.

He opened the door on to a wall of cameras. A storm of blue flashes. Blurred hands, clicks, whirrs, questions, voices calling his name, this way, that way, an outdoor microphone like a dead animal hanging over his head. He slammed the door just before the first foot jammed in the crack, and rattled the chain into the slot.

Danny had come to the door of the living room. 'Get back inside,' Tom said. 'I'm going to check the back.'

He ran downstairs and into the kitchen, feeling horribly exposed in the lighted room. But the door *was* locked, and, as far as he could see, pressing his cheek against the cold glass, there was nobody in the garden or on the riverside path. He drew the curtains, and stood, for a moment, with his eyes closed. The cameras had shaken him. Those whirrs and clicks were like the shards on a beetle's wings rubbing together. And the lenses. It was like being surrounded by insects. It was easier to believe there was a swarm of killer bees out there, than to believe they were human beings.

The phone rang. He snatched it up, thinking this must be Martha at last, but instead an unknown man's voice, wheedling, plausible, asked him to come to the door to be interviewed. He put the phone down without replying, and immediately it rang again. He couldn't disconnect it because of Martha. Slowly, he went back upstairs, feeling that for the first time in his life he understood what it was to be hunted. He was trying, through the pain in his hand, to keep calm, to think straight. He couldn't assume they knew Danny was in the house. Obviously they had a pretty good idea, or they wouldn't be out there, but they might not *know*. And until he was sure that Danny's identity as Ian Wilkinson had been blown, he couldn't do anything to jeopardize it. He needed to talk to Martha.

Danny was standing by the fireplace when he came in.

'How many?' he asked.

'Ten, fifteen? I don't know.'

Danny managed a smile. 'I don't think Ian Wilkinson's got very long to live, do you?'

'No, probably not.'

Danny shrugged. 'Doesn't matter. Never liked the guy anyway.'

He seemed to be pulling out of it. Tom wondered how much – if any of it – he remembered. 'I'll make some coffee,' he said.

The phone rang. They looked at each other, waiting for the answering machine to click in.

As soon as he heard Martha's voice, Tom snatched the phone up and began gabbling an explanation.

'Why don't you phone the police?' she said. 'There's no point hiding anything about Danny now. They must be causing an obstruction, and even if they aren't you can say they are.' She sounded entirely calm. 'I'll be round as soon as I can.'

'How long?'

'Twenty minutes.'

She rang off, leaving Tom feeling that he'd over-reacted. He phoned the police and explained the situation to a lethargic desk sergeant, who seemed inclined to take a long statement over the phone. Tom cut him short and put the phone down, with very little hope that any action would be taken. 'They'll be here soon.'

And then, because the feeling of being a rat in a trap was more than he could bear, he went to the other end of the living room and pulled the curtain aside. For a second there was no response, then another explosion of blue flashes. The hell he was overreacting. They were over the railings and into the forecourt now, lenses pressed against the window. He looked at Danny, who'd followed him across the room. 'Well,' he said, with an attempt at cheerfulness. 'At least it's not petrol bombs.'

Danny had gone white. 'It will be by the time they've finished.' He caught Tom's expression. 'Oh, c'mon, there's plenty of people hate me enough for that.'

Martha arrived fifteen minutes later, banging with her clenched fists on the door and shouting her name. She almost fell into the hall, then helped Tom to force the door closed behind her. Never had the smell of cigarettes and industrial-strength peppermints been more welcome.

'So what's all this, then, Danny?' she demanded.

Danny's voice shot up into a pubescent register. 'It's not my fault. I was followed. I came back here because I didn't want to lead them home.'

'Have you told anybody?'

'*No.*'

Martha threw down her bag. 'Well, somebody did.'

'You don't think it's just guess work?' Tom said.

'No. They're not parked out there on the off-chance. They *know.*'

'It doesn't matter how they found out,' Danny said. 'They're there.'

'It bloody does matter,' Martha said. 'Do you know how much work went into supplying you with a new identity?'

She doesn't want to lose him, Tom thought. And she knows she has.

'Did you phone the police?' Martha asked.

'Yes. I told them about Danny. They should be on their way.'

The next twenty minutes were like saying goodbye on a station platform. A limbo state in which nothing meaningful can be done or said, it's already too late, and yet the other person's still there, and one longs for, and dreads, the moment of actual severance. Neither Tom nor Martha could have the conversation with Danny that each of them wanted, and neither, in front of him, could they say anything useful to each other.

'Where will they take me?' Danny asked.

'Somewhere safe tonight, then probably down south.'

'London?'

'Perhaps. I don't know.'

'You'll write to me, won't you?'

'Yes, probably care of your new probation officer. I won't necessarily know your new name. But you ought to be all right transferring to another university and all that, once they've got the papers sorted out.'

A short silence. 'Danny, would you mind if I had a few minutes alone with Martha?' Tom asked.

'No, of course not.'

Martha looked surprised, but got up immediately and went into the hall. They left the door open.

'Look, Martha, all this stuff about transferring between universities is cloud cuckoo land. He needs to be in hospital.'

She peered through the open door. 'He seems all right. Well. In the circumstances.'

'He's pulling out of it now, but he has been very bad, he shouldn't be left on his own.'

'Well, he won't be alone tonight, because I'll stay with him. And I'll pass on what you've said. I can't do more than that, and I can't guarantee anybody'll listen.'

'That'll have to do, then. It's not enough.'

It wasn't enough because he hadn't said enough. He was shielding Danny in ways he had no time to think about.

'Tom, are you saying he needs to be in a secure hospital facility? Because if you are, you know what that means, don't you? The Home Office is going to rescind his parole.'

'Yes, I know.' He glanced at Danny, who seemed

to be aware of being observed, and turned to look at him. 'No,' he said. 'I'm not saying that.'

In the silence that followed, they heard the shriek of a police siren. Martha said, 'That's them now. We'll need a coat or something to put over his head.'

Tom fetched his coat from behind the utility-room door. It was the one he'd been wearing when he and Lauren went for that walk along the river path, and, as he took it from the peg, a powerful smell of river mud filled the room. He never had remembered to have it cleaned. He took it back upstairs with him. 'Here,' he said. 'This'll do.'

A fist banged on the door and Martha went to open it. Suddenly the hall was full of policemen in uniform, radios crackling at their hips.

'Don't worry about that lot, sir,' an inspector said, pushing his way to the front. 'We can't shift them altogether, but we'll get them moved to the end of the street. And if you have any more bother just give us a ring.'

A policeman waited, looking over his shoulder, one hand on the half-open door.

'I'll have to go, Tom,' Martha said, raising her face to be kissed.

'Good luck, Danny,' Tom said, handing him the coat.

Danny smiled. 'I seem to make a habit of walking off with your coat.'

'Keep it this time.'

Martha ran to get her bag and came back hitching it over her shoulder, looking pale and excited in a slightly shame-faced way. Tom watched a policeman wrap Danny's head in the black folds of the coat. 'Don't worry,' he said. 'It's only till they get you into the car.'

'Right, then!'

The inspector nodded to the man by the door. And then they all barged out into a chaos of clicks, whirrs, shouts and flashes. Martha followed. Tom saw her walk round the car and get in the other side, while one of the policemen, shielding Danny's head with his hand, pushed him down on to the back seat.

The car nosed forward, journalists trotting alongside, shouting questions, holding cameras to the windows. The remaining policemen forced them back. Thwarted, they came running back to Tom, who nipped into the house and slammed the door in their faces. He didn't see the car pull away, accelerate and disappear round a bend in the road.

Shouts from the street as the policemen persuaded the press to move further away. Tom leant against the door, his burnt hand pressed into his armpit, gasping for breath as if he'd just returned from a run, and stared at the space where Danny had been.

TWENTY-TWO

After a few minutes he pulled himself together, went upstairs to the bathroom and held his hand under a stream of cold water for a full ten minutes. It should have been done immediately, of course, but even now it might help to minimize the damage. Turning off the tap, clumsily, with his left hand, he inspected the burnt areas.

The fingers were swollen and shiny, but the only real injury was to the palm of the hand, which was badly blistered, though as far as he could tell all the blisters were intact. It wasn't possible to go to the hospital. He could imagine what the headlines would be if he turned up in the casualty department now. He had no choice but to do the job himself. It was difficult, working only with his left hand, but he padded the burnt area well, and managed to wind clear tape round his hand to keep the wads of lint and gauze in place. Then he took painkillers and sleeping tablets, and crashed out on the bed.

It was late morning when he woke. After lying for a few minutes, blinking, he crawled out of bed, cradling his burnt hand, and went across to the window, where he peered through a crack in the curtains, trying to make out whether the reporters had gone, or merely retreated to the end of the street. He couldn't see anybody, except Mrs Broadbent setting off for the shops, leaning heavily on her trolley, which was really a sort of disguised Black Watch tartan Zimmer frame. After trundling a few yards down the street, she turned and went back, trying the door handle to make sure that it was locked. And immediately Tom remembered another old lady who'd done exactly that, and died because of it.

He spent the rest of the morning, and most of the afternoon, creeping round the house, or listening to messages on the answering machine. The phone rang every two or three minutes, some calls from journalists wanting to talk about Danny, others from friends who'd heard the news of his split with Lauren. He would have to return those calls, but he didn't feel like doing it now. The person he most wanted to hear from was Martha, but she didn't ring, too busy handing Danny over to whoever was going to supervise him through the next stage of his life. The next identity.

After lunch, he tried to do some work on the book, but could neither hold a pen nor type for very long. What he really needed was to get away, and towards evening he left the house by the back way, along the river path, walked into town and took the train to Alnmouth, where he spent the night. Next morning, he hired a car and set off for Hadrian's Wall.

His plan was to walk along the Wall westwards from Housesteads over Cuddy's Crags, Hotbank Crags, Milking Gap, high above the steely waters of Crag Lough, and on to Peel Crags and Winshields. But by the time he reached Vindolanda it was blowing a gale. He persevered for a time, staggering in the gusts, but the wind threatened to blow him off the Wall, and along with other disappointed walkers he was obliged to turn back.

Instead, he drove to the coast, parked the car and walked across the causeway to Holy Island. It was low tide. The flat, shining, level sands stretched out for miles on either side of the road. It was difficult to believe that at high tide the ground he was walking on would be fifteen feet below the sea.

The causeway was longer than he'd remembered. He was sweating by the time he reached the sign by the side of the road: WELCOME TO THE HOLY ISLAND OF LINDISFARNE. He climbed the steep hill on the other side, following a path that ran between sand dunes crowned by plumes of bleached marram grass.

He walked all the way round the island, looking at the cormorants that lined the cliffs on the seaward side, their black wings hung out to dry. Thirteen hundred years ago, Eadfrith and Billfrith, Dark Age scribes, had used those birds to illuminate the Lindisfarne Gospels, thick, supple, snake-like necks coiled around the initial pages of St Matthew and St John. Yet surely then, as now, they must have seemed ominous, those black shapes against the sky, harbingers of death.

At lunchtime he went to the nearest pub, ate sandwiches, drank rather too much beer and lingered by the fireside, talking to a middle-aged couple who were on a walking holiday and, like him, had been forced to abandon their original plan of walking along the Wall. Eventually they left, saying they would try again tomorrow, and he sat on by the fire, sinking into a bovine reverie as the warmth lulled the pain in his hand to sleep.

When, finally, he left the pub, he discovered that a sea fret had blown in across the island, and the sand dunes were half hidden in drifting veils of vapour. He made slow progress. His joints had stiffened during the long rest by the fire, and at times he seemed to be merely hobbling along. The sea fret had brought with it a drop in temperature, and the palm of his hand prickled and burned.

He was less than halfway across the causeway when the mist thickened. Looking round, he saw that the island had vanished, and that the coast ahead of him was no more than a dark smudge in the all-encompassing white. Only the midway refuge, a hundred yards ahead, was still visible. He wondered if he should turn back, but that would mean spending the night on the island, and although, at this time of year, it would be easy to get a room, the prospect made him feel claustrophobic. He peered out over the water, trying to judge how long it would be to high tide. The sea had another nine or ten feet to rise before it even lipped the edges of the road. Plenty of time.

The mist was damp. The surface hairs on his woollen sweater were matted with drops of moisture, though it had not rained. Now and then, a wave lifted the masses of bladderwrack on the beach, and let them fall again, releasing a pungent smell of salt water and decay. His footsteps echoed, seeming to bounce back at him from the wall of mist. It was easy to imagine that somebody else was out there, walking towards him. This was a place for the unexpected, the near-miraculous meeting. It would not have surprised him to see Danny emerge from the sea fret, with that curious walk of his, head down, hands deep in his pockets, striding along as if he had all the space in the world. As if he were walking through some internal landscape, for where, in the confined places of his upbringing, could he ever have learnt to walk like that?

Tom stopped to look out over the water. He was thinking that Danny had won. That in the end, like Angus, like no doubt countless other people whose names he didn't know, he'd bent the rules for Danny. Two nights ago – only two nights, it seemed much longer than that – he'd seen Danny lapse into a border-line psychotic state, and Tom's vague general warning to Martha had not gone nearly far enough. He knew that if, at some future time, Danny were to set a fire in which somebody died, his silence on that night would return to haunt him. He knew what he should have done. Only, at the crucial moment, Danny had turned to look at him, and it had not seemed possible to betray him.

A wave seethed in the bladderwrack at his feet. He looked around and saw that the tide was racing in fast, the last few yards of sand disappearing faster than he would have believed possible. Already it was too late to go back to the refuge, far, far too late to return to the island. He had no choice but to go on. Heart thudding against his ribs, he broke into a run. Surges of water, laced with foam, flooded the road in front of him. He splashed through them, gagging from the effort.

Then, suddenly, the ground was dry again. He slowed to a walk, legs trembling, feeling that he'd panicked for no reason. Though when he looked back, he saw that the road ran straight into the sea. The whole central section of the causeway had disappeared under the water. Only the refuge, high on its stilts, becoming clearer, minute by minute, as the mists round Lindisfarne receded, was left to look out over the swirling tide.

A week after he got back home, Tom woke to a new noise. The light bulb in the kitchen was swinging on the end of its flex. He went to the front door and looked out, but could see nothing.

After breakfast, he ventured into the decaying hinterland of warehouses, sheds and factories, and saw a bright-yellow crane with a huge metal ball dangling from its jib. As he watched, the crane reversed, the ball swung and struck the side of a building, the blow sending spasmodic jerks rattling up the chain. Plaster and brick dust leaked from the open wound. Clumsily, the crane reversed. Another shock, another succession of shudders running up the chain. This time a whole section of the wall collapsed.

He spent the next few weeks living on the edge of a building site, doors and windows kept shut against the noise and dust. Curiously the work going on around him seemed to lift his mood. He worked steadily on the book, amazed he could work at all, for whenever he lifted his eyes from the screen he was aware of Lauren's absence. Soon he was going to have to decide what to do about the house – what to do with himself – but the book came first.

Martha read it chapter by chapter, commented, commented again on the next draft. They met, now, several times a week, developing a habit of takeaway suppers with cans of beer. When she was there the house seemed less hollow. Always, as soon as he was alone, the absence rushed in, though, as time went by, it became more difficult to say whether the absence was Lauren's, or Martha's.

Lauren, he discovered from Roddy and Angela who kept in touch with her, was living with somebody called Francis. This happened so quickly it was obvious that Francis had been waiting in the wings. But at least Lauren's desire to enjoy her new life unencumbered expedited the divorce. Only when he had the piece of paper in his hand did Tom start to feel free.

Winter closed in, icy winds blowing flurries of stinging snow off the river. The pleasure of pulling on an old, warm, well-trusted sweater became nightly more apparent. The time came when the evening's talk drifted into silence, and it seemed merely silly for Martha to go home. They took the relationship one day at a time, neither of them assuming it would necessarily last, though they did suit each other, physically and in every other way, surprisingly well.

Gradually life settled into a new pattern. All around Tom's street, shops, restaurants and hotels were springing up. Even the river changed. The crumbling jetties and quays were demolished, paths laid, trees planted. One night, looking over the railings at the place where shopping trolleys used to go to die, Tom saw what he took to be a large rat lolloping along the bank. But then he realized it was too big, and anyway rats don't lollop. Another shadowy creature joined the first. He glimpsed wet hair roughed up into spikes, a moist nostril questioning the air. Otters. He could hardly believe it. Otters on the Tyne.

Throughout all this time, Danny neither wrote nor

phoned. Martha had news of him occasionally, though only indirectly, through his new probation officer. Tom wasn't surprised by his silence. This, rather than any 'gimmick' of throwing cassettes on to a fire, was Danny's way of burning the tapes.

But then one day, without warning, he saw him again. Tom had gone to the University of Wessex to give a talk on the Youth Violence Project. He arrived in the late afternoon and, after leaving his bag in the hall of residence where he was going to spend the night, was taken straight to the teaching block.

The lecture theatre was large, with the platform raised well above the auditorium. The lights were too bright for Tom's taste, and at first he couldn't see the audience at all, except as a blur of faces. Gradually, his eyes adjusted to the glare and he thought he saw a familiar face at the end of the second row on the left.

Danny. Or a young man who looked like Danny. He couldn't be sure.

He sat, sipping water, listening to the introduction, working out how good the acoustics were, how good the microphones were. When he stood up to speak, he gazed around deliberately for a second, trying to see into the darkness of the auditorium, but he couldn't. The figure remained shadowy, elusive. As soon as Tom began to speak he forgot about him, in the need to make contact with this large, intent, but, at seven thirty in the evening, inevitably jaded audience.

The talk went well. He'd given similar talks many

times before, and could do it, now, almost on automatic pilot. When the time came for questions, he asked for the house lights to be raised, and there, unmistakably, was Danny. He'd been almost sure, but even so the sight of him was a shock. He stumbled over the answer to the first question, but recovered quickly.

After the questions, there were glasses of wine on a table in the foyer. Tom talked to various people who asked questions or made comments, aware all the time of Danny, who was leaning against a notice-board, a backdrop of many-coloured pieces of paper forming a jigsaw round his head. A rather aggressive young woman with dead black hair accused Tom of patronizing the people he spoke about. He'd given the entire talk, she said, without once seeming to be aware that there might be people in the audience who'd been in young offenders' institutions. Tom explained courteously that he'd made no assumptions at all about the audience, beyond their willingness to listen.

'You're just exploiting them,' she said, her nose-stud popping out with the force of her convictions.

'I didn't think he was exploiting them,' Danny said, coming up to join them.

'How would you know?' She stared Danny in the eye, then, when he didn't blink or move, turned on her heel and strode away.

'She did six months for dealing,' Danny said. 'It's her main claim to fame round here.'

Tom looked round, and realized that the audience was drifting away. He said goodnight to his host, who was worried he might not find his way back to the hall of residence.

'It's all right,' Danny said. 'I'll show him the way.'

They went out into the gardens. A few hundred yards away the student bar was full of lights and music. People sat at tables outside, or spread out on to the grass, testing it before they sat down.

Earlier in the evening there'd been a shower of rain, enough to release the smell of lilacs from the bushes behind them. Danny reached up and caught a branch, sending a cascade of raindrops over his face and hair.

'How are you?' he asked, before Tom could speak.

'Pretty well, and you?'

'Not so bad.'

No explanation for his long silence, but then none was required. They had slipped back into the intimacy of their first meeting.

'Whereabouts are you on your course?'

'Finals this year.'

'And then?'

'I'm doing the MA in writing. It's been a bit of a rush getting a portfolio together, but Angus has been very good.'

'Angus MacDonald? You got in touch?'

A stab of jealousy that amazed him. He would have said he was incapable of such a reaction, and yet jealousy was unmistakably what he felt. Just as Martha would be jealous when he told her about this meeting. He thought about it, and decided to be amused. It was Danny's gift.

'I went on one of his courses,' Danny was saying. 'Very salutary.' He didn't say how.

Tom turned to look back the way they'd come. The lights in the teaching block were being switched off, one by one. Against the night sky, the building looked like a huge liner sinking, the lights, first on one deck, then another, going out, until everything was dark.

'I won't ask you your new name,' he said, smiling.

'No, better not. I've made up my mind about one thing though.' He was looking towards the bar with its crowds and music. 'If it happens again, I won't run. There has to be a time when you say: "No, I'm just not running any more."'

Tom nodded. 'I think that's right.'

'Well.' A shadowy smile. 'It's been nice seeing you again.'

'How are you, really?'

'I get by.' He hesitated. 'I don't fight her now. She's got a right to quite a few of my brain cells.'

They'd come to a fork in the path. 'You're over there,' Danny said, pointing. 'Keep on the path. It brings you right round to the front door.'

They shook hands. Tom watched him walk across the grass to the bar. As he reached the terrace, a group of people sitting at one of the tables called out a name that Tom convinced himself he hadn't heard, and Danny went over to join them. One of the girls kissed him. A young man threw a proprietorial arm across his shoulder. Tom wondered if either of them knew who he was.

But no. Danny would have learnt to take what he wanted and keep a safe distance. There was no limit to what Danny might learn.

And that's the way it has to be, Tom thought. He was looking at success. Precarious, shadowed, ambiguous, but worth having nevertheless. The only possible good outcome.

The smell of lilacs was overwhelming. Tom closed his eyes for a moment, shutting out the sight of Danny and his friends, and saw instead, with almost visionary clarity, a woman with white hair walking down a garden path, five or six cats following her, their tails raised in greeting. She lifted a handful of dry cornflakes to her mouth and ate them, peering into the sun she could hardly see, enjoying its warmth on her face.

There, under the lilacs, with nobody to care or know, he stood for a moment in silence, remembering Lizzie Parks.